The Cadillac Diet

The Cadillac Diet

or

An Act of God

is

a

Hard Act to Follow

m. lewis

Writers Club Press
San Jose New York Lincoln Shanghai

The Cadillac Diet
or An Act of God is a Hard Act to Follow

Writers Club Press
an imprint of iUniverse.com, Inc.

For information address:
iUniverse.com, Inc.
5220 S 16th, Ste. 200
Lincoln, NE 68512
www.iuniverse.com

Many occurrences herein may have been inspired by actual events. The
characters are fictional and/or composites. Any resemblance to actual persons
living, dead or born again is strictly co-incidental. Some parts of the story
may be inappropriate for those under 18 years of age.

ISBN: 0-595-18290-9

Printed in the United States of America

Epigraph

A PROPHET IS NOT WITHOUT HONOR

EXCEPT

IN HIS OWN COUNTRY

&

IN HIS OWN HOUSE

&

IN HIS OWN FAMILY

MATTHEW 13:57

Contents

Acknowledgements

Thanks to my Mother, Sallie Lewis of Houston, for instilling in me the desire to learn about Spirit. Thanks to my friend and partner, Diane Maurno, for providing the means and the time and place (Montreal) for me to complete this work. She is the true artist! Also, thanks to the incredible Mr. Silver (D.B. Meyers) for giving me a computer in L.A. upon which this work was completed. Thanks, also, to the thousands of Souls who've inspired me.

Glory to God

List of Contributors

Prologue

Signs and wondrous things were being rumoured all over this small north Florida town. Something had happened down near the huge cross that dominated the horizon on the grounds of the old Spanish cemetery. The setting for this cross was beautiful and historically significant. It sits at the edge of a lagoon that opens up to the intra-coastal waterway between the mainland and the barrier islands near a neck of water that runs out to the broad deep Atlantic and across to the old world. To this very point the earliest Spanish explorers had come, bringing before them the sign of the cross. In those days there had been a village on this spot, recorded as Hochelaga. It was home to a group of Native Americans called the Timucua. Until the moment of the European landing, the Timucua had considered themselves a chosen people. THE People. Only now would they discover they were mere savages. They had what they needed. They received fish from the sea and shellfish from the tidal pools. Fruit and vegetables and meat came from the land. The land also furnished the Timucua with logs and hides and palm thatches for housing. They had a unique way of dealing with the, then omni-present, threat of alligators. They would sharpen a long stout wooden pole. Several men would wield this and ram it deep into the innards of an open mouthed, hissing 'gator. These people were also quite tall. The men were, on average, over 7 feet and the women 6 feet. The average Spanish male of that period was about 5 feet, 4 inches. These things are known from Spanish accounts of the day as there are no known surviving Timucuans. It wasn't 'gators or hurricanes that got them. It was, more accurately, the cross.

Now this towering stainless steel cross erected to commemorate the European conquest of the new world became the source of gossip in town as it was being whispered that, recently, someone here had seen the face of Jesus appear in the sky just above the cross.

CHAPTER ONE

Phat Cadillac

Michael Wade had heard these rumors. They concerned him little at present. He had only been in this tiny town of several thousand souls for a short while…and…his cash was running low. He needed a job. He didn't want to work in the much larger city of Jacksonville that existed thirty miles further north. He disliked any city over 100,000 people. Although, he had lived in the madness of Miami for many years; only recently escaping. Make the jump to Jax? No. He'd see what employment was available here.

On this Monday morning in early June, he sits on the attractive, though inexpensive, hexagonal oriental rug in the middle of his living room. The sun sends bright splashes of radiance pouring through the four angled panels of the bay window and illuminates the classified section of the San Jacinto Light that's spread out before him. A large display ad catches his eye. How could it not? It was the biggest ad in the tiny towns tiny paper.

SALESMAN NEEDED
No Experience Necessary!!
$50,000 First Year
Realistically!!
Call
Bentley Harrison III
at
Harrison Cadillac

$50,000. That would be nice.

That would definitely help Michael's financial situation. He had one thing the ad stated—no experience. Never mind that he'd never had a pleasant encounter with any car salesperson. Never mind that he had never sold anything so large and expensive as an automobile.

$50,000. That would be nice. After all, he has to support his teen-age son and himself.

He dials the number and is immediately put through to Mr. Harrison-the Third. How many are there? A slightly southern twang tells Michael that Mr. Harrison, the Third, is probably a local product. Maybe Georgia. He invites Michael for an interview at the showroom tomorrow at 2 p.m.

'What to wear, what to wear…' Michael is thinking the next day as he prepares for the interview. God, the idea of working for someone else is repellent to him. In his forty years on earth, twenty have been spent in pursuit of the dollar. To be sure, he had often worked for others. Making other people money. But he was most happy whenever he spun off to do his own business.

His most recent venture had been a small shop in the Coconut Grove section of Miami selling private label personal care products like shampoos, soaps, brushes, massage oils, etc…He had managed to hold his head above water for several years doing this and he really had enjoyed the lushness of the Grove and being just two blocks from the ocean. Large bodies of water had always held a certain powerful attraction for him. They had a calming, enriching effect on him. But ever since Hurricane Andrew in '92 wiped out his under-insured stock, he had found it tougher and tougher to make a livable profit. Plus 'the Grove', and all of south Florida, had undergone dramatic changes in recent times. Now there were huge mall stores with which he had to compete. They carried products as good as his and in greater profusion. His suppliers had gone up on their prices while the heavily bankrolled mall stores could hold gigantic discount sales. Over the years, his customer base had been local, year-round residents who knew him and liked him. The seasonal tourist trade also comprised a sizable portion of his business. Many of the locals had begun moving away to places less congested and less vulnerable to seasonal storms. He hadn't been able to replace these lost customers with the newer more affluent types that had come with the transition of the Grove from its artist colony roots to its new upscale, trendy image. Many of the newcomers preferred shopping in stores owned by people with Spanish surnames. Coconut Grove property had gone up in value so it wasn't unexpected when his rent continued to escalate even as his sales volume declined. The house he had bought on Kumquat Avenue many years ago had originally cost him only $50,000. It was definitely worth more now; but taxes were eating him up. When he had looked around for another house he found that anything worthwhile was in the ¼ million dollar range.

He probably would have persevered there if another aspect of Miami hadn't have become so prevalent. Violence. Violence had increased to epidemic proportions. Indeed it permeated Miami and most large American cities. The past couple of years it had gotten closer and closer and much more personal. He was reflecting one night back then and started making a list of all the people he personally knew that had been the victims of crime. It astonished him. 27 people had been robbed on the street or in their homes. 6 people had their cars stolen. There were 4 people who'd been shot and lived and 3 who'd been murdered and died. His own store had been broken into twice that very year. The final nail in the coffin was pounded home when he picked up the newspaper one day and read of the death of a beautiful young woman he had only recently met. He had thought seriously of striking up a relationship with her. Then, there she was. She and two of her friends. On the front page. Dead. They had all been executed. Their brains were blown out. Drugs? Jealousy? He nor the police would ever find out. Soon his son would be coming to live with him. He decided to get out.

A friend told him about a pretty little historic town in north Florida. Until then he didn't know if San Jacinto was on the east coast or the west coast of Florida. It turned out to be on the right coast and on the ocean. And historic? In Florida? Anything in Miami over fifty was declared 'historic'. He went up to check it out and discovered a very pretty little town. He had visions of opening a small shop downtown where the tourists came to see the old buildings of one of the earliest European colonies in the new world. 'Wouldn't the people in Boston be surprised about this', he thought. He found a cute house just a short walk from the downtown plaza and arranged to buy it. All this had been contingent on his unloading his store and house in Miami He sold his store for basically the wholesale cost of his goods. He got close to market value for his house but the bulk of those funds disappeared at a far greater pace than he had anticipated. At least he was happy with the cost of his new home in San Jacinto. A comparable house in south Florida would have cost him several times the price. Moving costs and the expense of bringing his son to live with him left him nervous about the immediate financial future.

Now here he is, after many years of independence, trying to figure out what to wear to an interview for work as a car salesman. This is crazy. He's thinking he should try to look like he could own a Cadillac. Yeah, that's it. He'll use the old 'bankers philosophy'. If you look like you don't need the money; they'll gladly give it to you. Perhaps if he appears to not need a job; he'll get one. As he first looks through his cramped closet and then the English armoire he had bought and refinished to supplement said closet; he selects a deep green wool double-breasted suit. He has a small selection of suits as he's really had limited use for them since he's dressed in the casual manner of a shopkeeper in a tropical climate for many years. What he does have is of excellent quality. Now he selects a tie. He lets the silks slip through his fingers and feels that one from Burberrys will do. It's a yellow-gold tone with subtle green teardrops that match the suit selection. A pale yellow dress shirt, deep green socks (adorned by a depiction of Atlas shouldering the world) and black wing tips complete the outfit that may land him this job in supercardom. Oh, God. It's been a while since he wore this particular suit. The jacket still fits but the pants are a bit snug. He looks to see what size are these? What size is he? In his teen years his slightly over 6-foot frame had worn 32x34 pants. As he'd gotten older and, he had to admit, a bit more sedentary he'd gone to a square 34x34. Now he's beginning to think he'll have to try a 36x34. The world turned upside down. There's no time for alterations or a crash diet. He has only thirty minutes to get to Harrison Cadillac.

Suck it up.

Suck it in.

Hook-snap.

He's in.

They're on.

For the first time he feels old. He's certainly older than he's ever been. He did have a fleeting brush with feeling older about three years ago when his girl friend, at the time, broke up laughing while he was engaged further south. He inquired if he'd hit a ticklish spot. No, she'd explained, he was losing some hair and she'd just noticed it.

Michael is trying to shed himself of all negative thought as he nears the Cadillac lot. He cruises the building a couple of times, slowly, as he reconnoiters the situation. He may look like he could own a Cadillac, but he doesn't. And he doesn't want them to know that he currently drives a Hyundai Elantra. Not a bad car; but it's no Cadillac. His family had owned Cadillacs for many years. He grew up riding in a '51. His family had bought it new and kept it until 1966. It had an actual ivory steering wheel. Additionally, it had electric windows, power, air, the whole bit. Cadillac had pioneered many of these features. He had always loved Cadillacs. Maybe he could sell them.

The dealership straddled both sides of San Jacinto Avenue. The west held the service bays and the east grounded the showroom. There is a long line of older cars, mostly Caddys, to the right of the showroom. In front of the showroom are the most handsome of the shiny new Cadillacs. They're carefully angled to attract the eye of the drivers of lesser cars as they pass by. To the left of the showroom are more rows of new Cadillacs. Across the street the service area abuts an administration building where the voluminous paperwork required of a new car purchase is filed away. He knows about that paperwork. Just prior to his having left Miami he had gotten his Elantra. He figured that he had better get a new car now. He had a business; an established residence and none of his financial problems were evident to any one but him. He had no idea what the near future might bring. He'd better get a car now while his paper self looked good to creditors. He wanted a vehicle with all the creature comforts, some size, and he wanted economy. Besides, they were just about begging people to buy the slow selling Hyundais. He had taken two newspapers and three books with him to enable him to wait out the dealers obligatory haggling. He had estimated his budget and wasn't going to buy or leave until he got the deal he was after. He was there for five hours. He got just what he had in mind. Now he was going to be on the other end.

Michael decides to take a left by the service building and park just out of sight of the main building. He walks over and slips on his jacket just before opening the showroom door.

"Hi, welcome to Harrison Cadillac!" says an attractive forty-something, tall, blond woman standing next to a podium just inside the entrance. The showroom is airy and light with several glass partitioned cubicles along the walls spreading both left and right from the greeters' podium. A telephone switchboard desk womanned by a young female attendant is several feet behind the greeter. Beyond that is a small but plush customer waiting area with sofa, end tables, lamp, coffee table and a large console style T.V...All this is done nicely in warm woods and wine colored fabrics. Michael guesses this is to keep the potential customer feeling at home until the crucial moment of truth. "Hi, I'm

Michael Wade to see Bentley Harrison the third. I have an appointment at two."

"Oh, you want JR. Have a seat and I'll get him for you." Michael notices that with the words JR the figures whose faces had begun to work their way towards him begin to recede. They slither much like the dark gnomes of the underworld in the movie 'Ghost'. 'Salesmen', he thinks, 'sniffing for fresh blood. And here comes their boss.' "Michael, hi. I'm JR Harrison. Come on back."

Bentley is a man of thirty-three years or so, maybe 5'10", immaculately dressed in a gray suit in the currently popular 4-button Lord Fauntleroy style. He even has on diamond studded cufflinks. On the way to JRs' office, Michael asks, "Are you Bentley and JR?"

"Yeah, my dad owns the place and even though he's the Second, he's senior to me. He and my mom have always called me JR. Short for Junior."

"If you're Junior and he's the Second, what's he called?" "Everyone just calls him Mr. H.. Here have a seat."

JR's office is at the rear of the bank of cubicles to the left of the front entrance. Of course, it's a much larger office than the open cubicles. It has a door behind which are done secret calculations, Michael figures. It also has blinds on the window for...said same purpose?

"Michael, tell me a little bit about yourself."

Michael recounts a shortened version of the odyssey that led him here. He finishes with,

"Sir, I really need this job to establish myself in this community. I need to make some money. And I love Cadillacs." He senses that JR could really care less about his words so he's surprised when JR says,

"Look, I like the way you dress. So, can you start tomorrow?" "Yes, sir. I can. What time?"

"First, take these papers out to the lounge and fill them out. Then bring them back to me and I'll give you your medical forms. Do you think you could go to our company doctor out at the beach and take a quick physical today?" "Yeah, sure. By the way, how is the pay structured here?" "Well, you make a minimum of $100.00 per car. Of course, we'll train you to maximize the profit on each sale and to get you started you get an advance of $100.00 per week. OK?"

"Yes, sir."

Sub One
Doctor, Please!

"Jesus. A hundred dollars per week. Oh well, that's just 'til I get the hang of it. I'll make it." Michael is muttering to himself as he drives out the coast road towards the doctors' office. As he drives he's noticing the nameplates on the rear of cars; the dealership ID that announces where each car has been bought. He's amazed to notice that fully half of the cars seem to have a Harrison Cadillac sticker on them. Not just on Cadillacs either. Many older and late models used cars of various manufacturers have this decal crowing from the back. Michael has no such free advertising on his car. He has always peeled them off and then rubbed an alcohol soaked rag over the spot to remove the glue left behind. He figured he had paid *them*; why should he do any free adverts for them?

At the doctors' office Michael fills out a little more paperwork. Have you ever had this; have you ever had that? No, no…He'd never really had any major health problems. He is somewhat uncomfortable that his waistline seems to be expanding; but that didn't overly concern him either He just didn't want to have to put out money to buy new clothes at this time.

"Mr. Wade? The doctor will see you now," a stubby little nurse with a cute face and a cute voice announces. She leads him to the exam room. Michael busies himself reading every surface in the room while waiting. He reads the labels on bottles, signs on the wall with health tips, diplomas, whatever's in sight. There's a light knock on the door and the nurse enters,

"Mr. Wade, let's get your height and weight," and she leads him a few feet away to a scale with attached height bar.

"Just step up here, please."

"What? With my shoes and everything on?"

"Yes, we make adjustments for that."

"I hope it's realistic. My wingtips alone probably weigh seven pounds."

As he's stepping off the scale the doctor rounds a corner and introduces himself while gazing at the chart the nurse has handed him,

"Mr. Wade. I'm Dr. Daniels. Hmmm…Harrison Cadillac, huh. Going to sell over there?"

"Yes, sir."

"That's where I got my STS. Nice car. Those boys sure keep me busy with new applicants."

"High turnover?"

"I don't know. Maybe they're just expanding. I only see them when they apply."

Michael surmises from the short clipped speech and the short clipped hair that Dr. Daniels has spent some time in the military. As they return to the exam room, the doctor says, "You know, from your height and weight, you could stand to lose about twenty pounds…"

"Twenty pounds! I didn't think I was that overweight."

"I've got a diet that's very easy to follow. I'm writing a book about it. Want to try it?"

"What's it like?"

"It's a high protein, low carb diet. Been very successful. You've got to drink a lot of water with it for two reasons. One to flush fat and toxins from the body and two, to make sure your kidneys don't dysfunction severely from the high amount of protein. The body, if deprived of carbohydrates, will consume the stored carbohydrates in your body. After that goes; then the fat begins to go. Now here's a copy of the diet and I'll go over it in a minute with you. First though, back to your physical. We'll need a urine sample."

"For what?", Michael says, feigning ignorance of the now standard drug tests required by just about all companies in the U.S. They'd have signs everywhere in the workplace. 'Just Say No to Drugs', 'Drug Free Workplace' and so on. Almost invariably some joker would alter these to read 'Just Say YO!' and 'Free Drug Workplace'. Michael liked to register his disapproval of such intrusion whenever prudent. Michael smoked pot and he liked it. He saw nothing wrong with it except that a million people were in jail for it. Billions of taxpayer dollars are spent each year in a futile and deadly effort to eradicate it. 'Idiots', he thought. He was certain that those that make the laws were not students of human nature. If they were they'd realize they could never stop people from trying to feel better. His own studies revealed that every culture and every period of recorded history would bear this out. Anyway, he was prepared. As the doctor exited so Michael could get some pee privacy, Michael extracted a thin, inch long plastic cylinder from his sock. It contained a readily available chemical mixture that, when mixed with urine, would render it drug free. And isn't that what they really wanted, drug free pee? The truth was many employers could care less about an employee's personal life, indeed, that's the American way. Do a good job and go home and relax. It was the insurance companies who had lead this pee test initiative and when an employer is told to do something by their insurance company, in this day and age, they do it. Dr. Daniels knocks and enters, "Well Michael, except for that twenty pounds, you seem quite fit. So, good luck at Cadillac. We'll send the results of your urinalysis to them in a few days. Now check with me in a couple of months so we can check your progress on that diet. Who knows, maybe you'll make it into my book!"

Crisp Asparagus

Take as much asparagus as you wish to serve and break off stems at the natural break point. Boil large pot water with steamer basket. When boiling add asparagus and cover. When brightest green (just a couple of minutes) remove basket with asparagus and plunge into bowl of room temp water.

Serve 'as is' or add fresh squeezed lemon juice and one of the following-shredded mint leaves, parsley, basil or chives.

Sub Two
Day One

The first day at the Cadillac store is an eye opener. He had been told to wear a nice suit. He did. It's black wool with a subtle pin stripe. He had no idea that he'd be starting his new 'career' performing manual labor in a black suit on a hot summer day. He feels that gym clothes would have been appropriate for his first morning's first task. He would learn that in many automobile dealerships there were crews of people to align all the cars just so. But not here. Not at Harrison Cadillac. Here the management had decided that sales people were, pretty much, free labor. The sales people straightened out all the cars on the lot first thing every morning. 'Perhaps they aren't familiar with the independent contractor laws', Michael thinks.

"OK, guys. Let's get this line straight!", yells the GM, Nero Fox. Nero is another nattily dressed southern accented man. He's about forty-five with high pompadoured gray hair.

"Sir, Michael Wade. I'm new. JR said to come out and help." "Hi there. Grab that '92 and pull'er into the front line." "Sir, don't you have people to do this? I thought I'd be selling…"

"This is a good way to learn your stock. Now grab that '92." "But sir, I've got on a black wool suit. I'll be soaked with sweat in no time."

"Tomorrow, wear an undershirt. Now grab that '92."

"Yessir."

So, what would become a daily grind began. Several men and one woman quickly scurrying around a blazing blacktop surface dashing in and out of first one car, then another. Pulling it up, pulling it back until Nero Fox is satisfied that the line is straight to within military standards.

As this task ends; Michael is relieved. He's so drenched with perspiration that he imagines this must be how Mary Jo Kopechne must have felt crushed beneath the accelerated power of gravity times water.

"Yo, guys-get back here!", JR yells as he crosses from the showroom to OK the alignment. "This doesn't look straight to me!"

And back they march to re-align the line. 'What is this? Some kind of car dealer machismo?', Michael wonders. As they're once again running in and out of cars, up, back, up again. From his rear, a less than manly voice is heard. It, too, bears a slight southern affectation…

"Hi, George Suffian. Don't worry, you'll get used to it." George continues as they quick step to the next group of cars to be moved,

"Where you from?"

"Miami. You?"

"Right here. Done a lot of traveling though."

"Where to?"

"San Francisco, Key West, Bangkok, New York…"

"Talk to you later!", Michael says as he dashes inside a blue Caddy. He thinks, 'Odd list of destinations.'

After the last vehicle is moved, Michael asks George, "Is it over yet?"

"Believe it or not; sometimes Mr. H will come out and have us do it a third time!"

"No? Are they sick?"

"Yes, Well, I've got a customer waiting. See you later," George says, as he sort of waddles away. George has an unusual gait. It's almost like a waddle with a wedgie. He's quite well dressed though. Tweed jacket, in the middle of summer no less, and not a bead of sweat on him. Pale pink shirt that picks up a light raspberry thread hiding in the brown tweed and a tie that reflects both colors. He looks prosperous with fewer of the outward manifestations of ostentatious display affected by JR and Nero Fox. A little classier, as it were. A voice intervenes upon Michael's observations, "He's gay, you know."

Michael is taken aback by this statement. The voice is from a man of about thirty-five years with thick sandy hair and collegiately rugged good looks. He reminds Michael of David Nelson from the old Ozzie and Harriet TV show.

"And you are?"

"Dave Nelson.

And you're the new guy."

"Right. Michael Wade." Michael extends his hand.

"George. He's gay, you know."

Michael plays dumb; mainly because he's known thousands of 'gay' people and figures as long as they don't butt-fuck him, who cares?

"You mean he's happy all the time?"

"No, man. A fudge packer."

"Oh, yeah. I remember seeing the fudge packing plant outside of town."

"No jerk. He's a homo."

"You sure? I mean; did he give you a blow job or something?"

"Hell no. Are you nuts?"

"No, I just don't believe in disseminating information without personal knowledge. So…I assumed that maybe you had some. Personal knowledge, that is."

"He's been de-semen-atin' all right. Just not in the normal receptacle."

"He looks to be quite well to do."

"Actually, he is. He's been here longer than anybody, has more regular customers, more referrals, more perks too. He's the only one, not in management, that gets a demo. Just about every month he sells more cars than anyone.Old man Harrison bought this lot from George's daddy about thirty years ago. Part of the deal was that George would have a place to work as long as he wanted."

"So, I guess he feels very comfortable here?"

"Yeah, like it was home.

Say, what desk did you pull?"

"JR gave me the one right in front of his office. I guess he wants to keep an eye on me."

Dave lets out a muffled chuckle,

"No, that's not it. No one else wants to sit behind Bobinsky."

"Who?"

"Paula Bobinsky. She was out there with us this morning. She drops farts wherever she goes. Usually SBDs. She even breaks it when she has customers in her booth. I think it's her equivalent of pissing on a tree to mark your territory."

"Great", Michael says sarcastically as he realizes he may have to dry off in a fart filled enclosure.

"Yeah, welcome to Harrison Cadillac."

"Thanks", Michael says a bit dejectedly as he heads toward his desk.

As he enters the showroom and reaches his assigned area, he notices a woman in his cubicle bent over his desk.

It's Bobinsky.

"Hi. Can I help you?"

"Oh, hi, Paula Bobinsky."

Michael sniffs the air and, thankfully, it's not too offensive,

"Yeah, I know."

"Oh yeah, how?"

"Oh, you just had that air about you."

"One of the guys finked on me, didn't they?"

"Let's just say they described you. Besides, you're the only female sales person, aren't you?"

"Yep, I am. Just using your calculator for a minute. Mind?"

"No. Go ahead. What happened to yours?"

"If you don't nail things down around here; they just walk off. And if you don't nail it; at least label it...Jeez. How can I fuck these people some more?...

I can jack up the add-ons. Yeah! That'll do it", Bobinsky finishes unconsciously. Michael notices as the short, slight shapeless figure of Bobinsky slides around to her side of the glass that her cheap sheer frock of opaque cotton reveals that she has on no underclothing. He thinks, 'Nudity and farts. Great sales tools.'.

Michael decides that he'll check out the smoking area.

He goes through the back door to what must be the former mechanics area of the store prior to the new service area across the street having been built. It's pretty disgusting at the present time. It's in distinct contrast to the customer waiting area of warm woods and wine colored fabrics just the other side of the door. This décor is more like 'early grease pit.' And just near the old rotted metallic rollup door that leads to the side street, opposite the used car lot, is the designated salesperson smoking area. There are a couple of smokers out there almost all of the time. The waiting part of car sales can be very boring. Right now there is a salesman there that Michael hasn't met. He's an olive skinned man. Puffing energetically. He looks to be about fifty with dark, slicked back, greasy hair and an, almost, beak-like proboscis. He seems nervous. Like a caged animal, he paces and puffs, while looking constantly toward the used cars to see if any customers have snuck onto the lot. Michael pulls out a Raleigh King and his trusty, smoke-colored Zippo and approaches,

"Hi, I'm Michael Wade. I just started here."

"Great. Another cherry to split up the pie. I don't know why they keep adding new people. First, that skag, Bobinsky and now you. Ever sell cars before?"

"No. I…"

"Just like I thought. What the hell you doin'? You think this is easy? Quit now. We don't need any more competition." Michael notices three Black guys on the used car lot washing the perfectly aligned vehicles and thinks he'll just finish his smoke over there. He figures this must be the detail crew. It can't hurt to get to know them and they must be friendlier than this fellow who just 'welcomed' him. As he gets closer, he realizes these faces are slightly familiar. He's seen them around his neighborhood of Washington Heights. Like Malcolm X used to say-if you want to find the Black section of town just look in the phone book under Lincoln. Or in this case, Washington. It is a mixed neighborhood and had been for a long time This is still a rare thing; but not here. He had heard that, long ago, Martin Luther King had marched in San Jacinto and sat-in at the Woolworth's lunch counter downtown. It is difficult to tell that Dr. King's presence has done much good. San Jacinto is still just one step removed from Plantationville. Maybe the King story is as accurate as Washington Heights is high. Face it. This is coastal Florida. If one stood on an orange crate; you could be designated the highest local point. "What's up guys?," Michael says using what his son has told him is a universal Black greeting.

"I'm Michael Wade," he says extending his hand to a very rotund, clean-shaven, young man in his twenties.

"I just started today."

The rotund young man seems startled at the offer of a hand,

"I'm Charles," he says slowly.

"This is Jones and this is Whitey."

Jones is another twenty-something young man. Only he's slightly built with a thin, almost pre-pubescent moustache. As Michael shakes the hand of Charles and then Jones, he senses reticence and sees a mix of mis-trust and con in their eyes. When he comes to Whitey; he notices a different attitude. Whitey is older; how old he can't tell. Whitey squares up and looks Michael cleanly in the eye. Their hands meet firmly and warmly,

"Hi, I'm Whitey Grayer. Thanks for saying 'hello.'

I hope you do well here."

It's only when Michael tries to be a little too hip that things get a bit confusing. Michael is trying to affect a 'solidarity' handshake by wrapping his four fingers around Whitey's thumb then backing out ending up in a reverse pike with a twist. The usual Black/White handshake confusion.

Michael says,

"I never know when to quit." They both crack a grin.

"Whitey, who's that guy, over there, in the smoking area?"

Whitey looks over.

"Oh. That's Nicholas Santos. He sells a lot to the Greek community here in town. He's been here quite a while."

"He seems a little negative."

"I don't think he's a happy man."

Just then, Michael is signaled (by the greeter at the side door of the showroom) that it's his turn for a customer. He says his goodbyes and thinks, as he dashes over, that this guy Whitey is pretty cool. He has a dignity that bears no relation to his position as a low-paid detail man. He likes what he feels from this man. And…what is that accent of his-Caribbean?

Michael's 'up' is just an older couple dreaming of a Cadillac. They have no financial means to trade in their old pick-up on anything on the lot. He knows they're just entertaining a fantasy. He really tries his best to be a dream facilitator. There's simply no way to get them into a newer car. Oh, well. Lunchtime…

Michael brought his own lunch. He goes back through the same door that leads to the smoking area. Except this time, he turns left towards the rear of the old mechanic's shop. He goes through a cheap core door to the employee lunch room. This is *no* cafeteria. *This* is an extension of the grease pit. It resembles a third world prison cell. It is *extremely* dirty and depressing. There is no way he can eat here. He decides to go outside to see if he can find a bench or something and at least enjoy some fresh air.

Out behind the 'pit' he spies a big shady oak. Underneath sits Whitey already breaking out the Tupperware®.

"Mr. Grayer. Mind if I infringe upon your solitude and join you for lunch."

"Sure. Have a crate and sit down."

Michael adjusts a blue milk crate and opens his bag of treats. Whitey asks,

"Whatcha got?"

"An avocado, romaine and tomato sandwich with a tarragon mayonnaise I whipped up."

"Kind of an A.R.T. 'stead of a BLT, huh?'

An amused Michael agrees,

"Yeah, I guess so. You?"

"Fettuccine al porcini."

"Ummm, cook that yourself?"

"Yeah. I find I can be more creative, get better nutrition, save time and a lot of money by bringing my own. Have you ever noticed how, in many office situations that half the day is spent with people contemplating their lunch hour? It says a lot about society today. Used to be you just brought your lunch and ate it. Not now. Listen and you'll hear people drone on about 'where will I go for lunch', 'well, where are you going to lunch?' And look at the choices they have-Mickey Ds, BK, Li'l Wendy. Or maybe a seafood option. Here we are on the coast of Florida and people go to Long Johns or Cap'n Ds and get some deep fried dead fish caught, god knows when, fifteen hundred miles away. Or the burger route gives you a greasy patty on white bread backed up by even greasier fries. Man, that's a heart attack waiting to happen. I mean they never ask you, 'would you like some nice leafy greens with that burger.' I just hope Canadian fries never get popular here. You ever have them?"

"No sir. What are they?"

"They serve'em with gravy and cheese poured on top. I guess they can handle it up there. They've got those hard cold winters to contend with. But down here, with our thin, hot tropical blood? Man, we'd have people dropping dead in the streets."

"That sounds about as sensible as them making the sales people wear suits and long sleeve shirts in a Florida summer. I mean this (Michael points to his own raiment) is a style of clothing that evolved out of medieval Europe. Tradition...I mean I've got nothing against tradition or even suits in the right environment...but this is stupid, Fries and suits. Stupid fucking tradition."

"So, What got you here…to San Jac…to Harrison Cadillac?"

"Quiet desperation, sir. And you?"

"When I got out of the navy; I was stationed in Jacksonville. I guess gravity kinda rolled me down here. I liked it…had sort of an islandy feel, long sandy beaches…got some history. What really clinched it though was that I met my wife, Mary Rose, here. One Sunday morning I wandered into a small Baptist church in the 'Heights' and heard this magnificent voice in the choir. That was Mary's voice. I conspired to meet her, we clicked and I never looked back."

"That's a neat story. Hope I find a Love like that here."

"Yeah, she's the Rose of my Heart."

"You know I live in the 'Heights'. Are you still over there?'

"Yeah, We've got a little place on Abbeyville Road called 'Mother Mary's Salvation Rib Station'. Bar-b-que and blues.

You oughta come by."

"White folks welcome?"

"Depends on the folks. You like ribs?"

"Indubitably!"

"Come on by. Mary runs the lunch trade and I handle the dinner crowd."

"If you own a restaurant; why do you work here too?"

"I'm a double safety man. You know. Like a man who wears suspenders and a belt. Just in case…gravy money."

"Abbeyville Road, huh? That sounds good. I love ribs and the blues."

Michael's thinking he should have asked Whitey what he's heard about the rumors going around town concerning the vision at the cross; but decides he'll wait until later at the rib place. The rest of the day is uneventful and sale-less. As Michael gets in his car to leave; George Suffian waves good-bye and says,

"You know, I've been to gay Paree, too!"

"Yes. So I heard."

Sub. Three
23rd Palm

Michael is anxious to get home and see his son, Skates. As the name implies, Skates is a Rollerblading®, skateboarding teen. Eighteen, to be exact. He's at the tail end of high school. He wears droopy drawers and huge floppy shirts. The better to skate in, my dear. And he's usually rolling on something-tires, Rollerblades®, little tiny skakeboard wheels, joints. Good kid. Good-natured. His father thinks he's sometimes a little too good natured as others, less worthy, want his attention and he obliges. Maybe he allowed some people to take advantage out of a need to acquire friends caused from his bickering parents broken home. Maybe it was partly because his dad had taught him to be as friendly as people would allow you to be. Michael Loved him. Whatever he is or would become; Michael had a role in creating Skates. He felt he had known his Spirit even before his birth. He even believed...no, he had no doubt, that his child had tried to enter his life through two other women before Skates' mother and both times he'd been aborted.

This was something that Michael didn't understand about the anti-abortion people. He had other names for them, too. Like the anti-after-you're-born people and the don't-kill 'em-'til-they're-alive people. Pro-life was far too non-descriptive and hypocritical. Didn't they know that the soul never dies? Didn't they know that the limited resources of planet earth could not forever sustain unlimited human population? He often thought of humans as present day dinosaurs. Masters of the Earth. Roaming and conquering at will; multiplying exponentially, out of control. He wondered how it would end. He'd heard one current theory that the dinosaurs died out due to a direct hit of an asteroid from the asteroid belt that crosses earth every twenty-six million years. Did that create a 'nuclear winter' or a 'greenhouse summer'? He did know that they died out after a dramatic climatic change and they were unable to react quickly enough. Still, he preferred the theory that dinosaurs had been so populous that they gagged on the methane created from their own excretory gases thus effectively altering their atmosphere into something unbreathable. With the big creatures out of the way; smaller creatures, like humans, were now able to emerge and expand. And here we are, he thought, creating our own dramatic, climatic changes with auto and industrial emissions. Will we destroy ourselves because we cannot and will not limit the degree of our excessive success? At times, Michael wished he had taken more of an interest in science. Someday soon, someone would have to harness the power of the sun. It powered almost everything on earth. Why not our precious personal transport machines? Michael loved the freedom and mobility of automobiles as much as anyone; but he felt guilty knowing that our marvelous machines were killing our air. And now, he was selling them.

Then Michael's thoughts shift back to the first time he met his son's Spirit. He had been alone, resting in a darkened room when an awareness occurred. It was difficult even for him to describe. He sensed, what visually appeared to be, an aerated bubble of barely discernible light hovering in the corner. There was communication of the silent type. No words, rather an acknowledgement of each other's Spirit. Michael, later, had forced himself to put the experience into words because that is how he could grasp it. Basically, the 'presence' indicated it would enter the world as his son. It took a couple of years and a couple of women for that to happen. When it did happen; he wasn't amazed at all. It was a given. That experience gave and still gives him much peace and joy about the nature of the universe. He has never related this to anyone except his son; who remembered nothing of it.

As he parks his car in front of his home at 23 Palm Avenue; he pauses just a moment to marvel at the compact cottage. From the outside, all that's visible is a time-darkened adobe wall with a twenty foot bamboo forest shooting up behind. As he opens the arched wooden gateway that leads to the back door and closes it; he now feels protected. A buffer from the outside world. A momentary resting place in eternity. The back yard has two aromatic and healing camphor trees, three large shady oaks and a scattering of plants, both potted and planted. There's aloe and bougainvillea and jasmine and camellias. There's a struggling banana tree and palms, short ones and taller, as well as a few that God or former residents supplied. A gated garden refuge.

Skates is in the living room,

"Hey Dad. How'd Cadillac go?"

"A little weird, but OK. I met this guy there who's got a rib place a few blocks away. Want to go?"

"No, not tonight. Richard and I are going to hang out downtown."

"Got any homework?"

"I did it already."

"So, how's summer school going?"

"I'll pass and then, I can get my diploma."

"Great!"

Michael didn't have many scholastic expectations of his son. He just wanted him to graduate. It wasn't that Skates was dumb; just doggedly individualistic; and rebellious. If a teacher rubbed him the wrong way; he would shut down and refuse to do well. Throughout his school years he'd done great when he had an exceptional teacher. Otherwise he fought failing. Michael recognized the good traits possessed by Skates. He was artistic and trusting of others. Skates would find his way and his Dad's Spirit was always there even through the many painful years they lived apart due to divorce. What Michael didn't get was why Skates' mother had waited until now to let Skates come live with him. Skates had just one year to go to finish school where he'd grown up. His mom had just recently married a very wealthy man and Michael's fortunes were headed downhill. Why now, when she could afford Skates a few luxuries and Michael could barely afford groceries? Oh well, he thought, just part of the grand plan (like dinosaur farts-the cosmic joke) for us to figure out. And we'd better laugh while we're doing it.

Michael changes his clothes and tells Skates,

"Skates, I'm going to run over to the rib joint.

See you later tonight, OK?"

"Sure Dad. Have a good time."

'Abbeyville and…what?' Michael wonders as he gets in his wine colored Elantra.

'Let's see. I guess I'll start at Central and work outward.' He slowly slips down Abbeyville, passing a few blocks of bass-blaring low riders, and just before town gives out he sees an oasis-like setting up ahead. It's a trim, stout, stained wooden building with smoke curling out of a red brick chimney. There's a smaller wooden building set further back that he figures must be a shed for firewood. The entire structure is set back from the road and looks well kept up. It's surrounded by lazy, shady palms and oaks. A sign directs cars to the back to reduce the parking lot look from the street. A larger carefully lettered sign announces that he has arrived at Mother Mary's Salvation Rib Station. Michael parks and walks in with a combination of anticipation and hesitation. Anticipation of juicy barbequed ribs. Hesitation because he isn't certain of how a white man will be received. What the heck, he has the invitation of the owner. Inside there's a twenty-foot wooden bar along the right-hand wall. Traditional red and white checkered table-cloths cover an assortment of tables leading back to a small stage with mikes, drums, speakers and a piano. A juke box in the middle of the left wall is belting out Muddy Waters' 'I'm Ready'. It feels good and it smells good with the flavorful smoky aroma of good wood burnin' for a good cause. The seats are occupied with faces of varying degrees of blackness. There are families, some older folks, some young teens and twenty-somethings (many wearing clothes similar to that which his son wears). There are several blue collar types, a few suits and some churchy women with starched dresses all having a pretty good time. Michael draws some polite turning of heads as his is the lone shiny white face to be seen. As he scans the room he sees no Whites and no Whitey. He approaches a woman behind the bar in a royal blue dress with hair high and coiffed. Her skin is the color of polished mahogany. Rather regal looking he thinks.

"Are you Mary?"

"Yes, sir. What can I get you?", she answers in a soft southern drawl.

"Well. I started working with your husband today and he invited me to drop on by. So, I did."

Mary's checking him out. Michael had changed into jeans and a tank top with a cap and sandals. His tank top has an African motif and his cap is cut from kinte cloth emulating west African tribal colors. He wore these to symbolize empathy. Whenever he did this, he often was looked at as just another White man usurping something of Black culture. Still, he persisted. He believes in the *human* race. After Mary's eyeballing, she says,

"Whitey should be here soon. Want a beer?"

"Yes, ma'm. How 'bout a Red Stripe?"

"You got it."

Mary didn't give herself away when she spoke. She was friendly but with a businesslike reserve-in case you turned out to be an asshole.

Momentarily, Whitey comes through the door with a guitar case slung over his back and a leather hat pulled down over short, tight dreads. He's no longer dressed in the plain brown jumpsuit required by his day gig. Now he appears to be a traveling troubadour. He sets down his case behind the bar and kisses Mary hello and smiles at Michael,

"Hey, glad you made it. Hungry?"

"Yes I am. I'm a rib fan."

"We do it a little bit different here. Our ribs are leaner than most. So the flavour has to come from the smoke, not the fat like most good meat. I start the fire each morning before six so the first batch is ready by lunch. I just let the flames lick at the meat; the smoke does the work. We always carry beef and pork, chicken and turkey. Once in a while we throw on lamb or game birds and we even do up fish every so often. No slave food though…like pig knuckles and such. We've got tangy and hot tomato based sauces; none of that Georgia mustard sauce though. We've got greens. Cookin' kind and salad kind. I believe in green things from the earth as much as Mr. H believes in green things from the bank."

Michael has to laugh at this as Whitey continues,

"We've got beans for the traditional minded and sweet potato pie. I'd suggest your meat of choice and a nice salad to go with that Red Stripe."

"Sold. I'll have some pork ribs and mixed greens."

Mary Rose goes back to the kitchen and returns with a heaping plateful of ribs and a beautiful salad that appears to have field greens and even some flowers in it. Considerably more than expected of the average rib joint. This causes Michael to exclaim,

"Hochelaga! Would you look at that."

Michael dives in and begins to clean his plate. The victuals are every bit as good as the visuals led him to believe. After enjoying the meal, Michael's attention returns to the proprietors,

"You know you've managed to combine the best of Black ribs with a European touch with that tasty mixed greens, dandelion thing. Very cool. I have to tell you, and I know this sounds racist, but it's so rare that I've liked white ribs. Black ribs are just better. There used to be this rib joint that I loved down in the 'Grove'; called Roy's Ribs. Many years ago down there, during the riots, old Roy refused to serve Whites-but he always served me 'cause I'd call him Mr. Roy. I loved those ribs so much I used to give them as gifts to people. And yours (he begins to break into a broad grin) Mr. And Mrs. Grayer are equally as good. Thank you."

"You are very welcome. Glad you liked 'em," says a grateful Whitey as Mary Rose approvingly beams by his side.

"Whitey, how the heck did you come by your name?"

"Mary, you want to tell him?"

"Sure. My husband's name is Louis Major Grayer. Near as we can figure that means Famous Important Man who's getting older…or at least Grayer." Mary says, ribbing her husband. Michael chimes in with,

"Michael means 'who is like God?'; but I was named after the Archangel. Wade means 'wanderer'. So, I'm an Archangel who wanders the earth."

"Anyway, when this man of mine first moved here everybody called him Major Grayer…because of the navy. 'Course he wasn't anything major in the navy, but he always commanded respect from everyone. People noticed that he did get treated differently, even by Whites. This awed some of the younger kids and they, kiddingly, started calling him Whitey."

"I liked the way it went with Grayer; so I kept it. And nothing's really black and white now, is it? I mean, just look around at the faces here. We're all called 'black'; but the English used to call people of India 'blacks'. Little did they know…"

Whitey points around the room,

"Every shade under the sun. Deep, almost blue-black, slanted oriental eyes, red tinged skin with an Indian forehead. All lumped together as 'Blacks'. Did you know that right here in San Jac was a fort, in Spanish times, that had only free Blacks and Indians as defenders. Of course, the Spanish put them way outside of town as the first line of defense, or slaughter, depending on the disposition of a particular battle. But they were free. And that was one thing the other colonial powers didn't abide. In case you're inclined to look for it; you won't find any markers or plaques. But it was there and the old Spanish archives confirm it. Shoot, the Seminoles were really a mix of Creeks and Blacks just trying to find a place to breathe. To do that, they had to take to the Everglades. The word Seminole means 'separatist'."

"I studied history in school but I've never heard about that fort or that bit about the Seminoles. For a guy like me; how do you think it feels being hated and feared by two-thirds of the world's people that aren't White?"

"That's only because you're apparently aware that there's more to life than race. Most Anglos that I've known, deep down, still wonder if Hitler wasn't correct about the 'master race'." At this, Whitey laughs upon seeing Michael's look of shock and surprise as Michael feels some shame for the race with which he is identified. Whitey continues, "I don't think racism will be eliminated until we're all blended into one color; and that may never happen. I mean, historically, different peoples seem to have evolved in different parts of the globe as they responded to variables in their particular environment. They may have all come 'out of Africa'. But they came in varied forms and at varied times. For instance, skin color is the body adjusting to the sun. Different pigments allow for different rates of absorption of vitamin D. I don't care who came first-whites, blacks, yellows, reds-whatever…the only people who research these things are trying to prove or dis-prove superiority. The point is that we all came to the party. We all have, can and will contribute something to the world. It will probably be something the world doesn't see. It may even be something *we* don't see. It may be a word whispered to someone at a critical time; it may be that you produce some progeny down the line that changes the course of history."

"Have you all ever been to the Yucatan?"

Both Whitey and Mary signify 'no'.

"Many years ago, I was walking in a jungle down there on a dirt path near the Rio Tonala. Tonala means 'magic' in Nahuatl and it was weird because the river was mud black, like 'black magic'. Anyway, all of a sudden I'm standing in front of this massive round stone head. It was, maybe, ten feet high. An ancient stone carving of an Olmec head. I'd seen them in pictures…but to come across one of these monoliths, face to face, in the middle of nowhere—to feel their power–it was awesome, incredible. What I'm getting to-is this; when I got back to the states I came across a book called 'They Came Before Columbus'. Its' premise is that Blacks were in the new world long before the Europeans. One thing offered as proof is these Olmec heads. Their facial features and head ornamentation can easily be interpreted as African in origin. After seeing one so close up; I can believe it."

"Yeah. Not too many people know of that book. But, like I said, the author was trying to prove or dis-prove superiority. It's important; but ultimately irrelevant. We have a saying where I come from–Columbus was a damn nasty liar."

Michael, Mary Rose and Whitey have a good chuckle over this and Michael asks,

"Where are you from?"

"A tiny speck in the Caribbean. You've never heard of it,"

Whitey says dismissively.

"You know, one of the few rap records I ever liked was 'Edutainment' by BDP."

"You listen to rap music?"

"Well, my son does. He turned me on to it. In there, they sing about some of the Egyptian pharaohs having been Black."

"True. Important for the world's education; but ultimately irrelevant. By the way, they aren't records anymore; they're CDs."

"CDs and cell phones. About the only things men want smaller."

"You know how crazy this race stuff is? I've got three types of blood running through my veins. Irish, Arawak Indian and African. But you ask anyone who I am and they'll say 'Black.'"

Mary turns to Whitey and says,

"Baby, why don't you get up on stage and give the folks a song?"

Whitey grabs his guitar and motions to his sidemen sitting at a table near the stage. One man picks up a bass and the other drops down at the drum kit. No piano tonight. They start off with a kind of tropical rock song. 'Trop Rock', Michael thinks. He is very impressed with Whitey's voice. It's a smooth baritone that's melodic and compelling. Michael thinks this must be an original tune and it's very good.

Mary Rose asks him,

"You want to dance?"

"Maybe after another Red Stripe."

"Here. On the house."

And even though Michael is somewhat intimidated about dancing here; he can't refuse the offer.

"Well, if you're gonna be that way about it…Come on, let's dance!" And they hit the floor.

Michael has never really been totally surrounded by Blacks. But, here he is dancing in a Black restaurant to a Black band with Black customers and his pasty white ass shaking out on the dance floor. After a while, he begins to look at his arms and wondering what's wrong with his skin. 'Why aren't I Black, too?' He is having a momentary fragmentary, miniscule taste of what it's like to be a minority. Most American Whites never even have this much experience with feeling different. He's getting the slightest taste of what it's like to be a Black person in America; except there's dancing.

So in a flurry of twirling swaying bodies and generally happy faces the night comes to an end. This is no all night joint. Working people have to rest. Ah, work-the curse of the dancing class. Checks and balances. Michael congratulates Whitey and thanks Mary Rose and takes his leave.

He decides to take the long way home. He takes the coast road and drives on the beach for a short distance just to feel the salt air and hear the surf tumble ashore. The moon hangs low over the ocean's horizon and he marvels at how wondrous it is that such a cold remote object can pull tides across the earth and fill his soul with such peace.

On the way back towards his home he passes the huge cross near the old mission. He notices about a dozen people huddled there around a small fire.

Praying?

Crash Cadillac Diet

This can take weight off fast. But, like anything worthwhile, it takes effort and discipline. Make it easier by consuming several glasses of water enhanced with lemon wedges. Take vitamins (at least a multi with lots of B). Don't exert yourself beyond your capacity. Consult your doctor, priest, rabbi or shaman.

Daily Ration

6-8 ozs. of protein. Could be lean meat (steak, chicken-even pork, cod, flounder or eggs).

4 servings of carbs. 1/3rd to ½ cup brown rice or pasta or whole grain bread.

8 ozs. no or low fat milk or no or low fat yogurt or sorbet.

2 servings of fruit. I.E.–one apple or one banana twice per day.

4 servings of veggies of ½ to 1 cup cooked or raw.

For variety, mix rice and veggies. Have veggies for breakfast. Anything to keep from going mad. Eat carbs early in the day and, if hungry at night, favor proteins.

CHAPTER TWO

Signs and Wonders

Michael continues going to Cadillac faithfully even though he's becoming increasingly doubtful about his prospects here. His sales suck. His lunchtime talks with Whitey, under the big oak, are becoming standard fare. One of these noons Whitey can tell that Michael's becoming concerned about his lack of production at the store.

"How ya doin' with your sales?"

"Pretty bad."

"Would you care for a tip or two?"

"Sure."

"When people come into a car dealership; especially a high dollar place like this; they expect to get screwed. They trust nobody and they're usually right. They don't know you and you don't know them. Plus, this is a small town. Lots of people are regulars here and they've already got their own particular sales person. So, you've got two things going for you. You trust people and you'd rather give someone the benefit of the doubt until they prove themselves otherwise. Right?"

"Yes. That's true."

"Secondly, you seem to have few, if any, prejudices and you like people. Right?"

"Also true."

"So, when you get an 'up' don't think about how much of a fish out of water you are here. Don't think about how little of this game you know. Don't think about how much money you need to make. Just think about meeting this person that just came through the door. Talk to them. Talk *about* them and their lives…like a TV interviewer might do. And–take the customers nobody else wants. A lot of Blacks drive Cadillacs and a lot of them walk right through those doors. Tell them you know me…that you hang out at Mother Mary's. Take the customers that aren't dressed so well…the ones the other sales people shy away from. Talk *to* people: don't *sell* to them. Ask them about their lives, their kids. They won't all buy; but it will pay off."

"Give me your tired, your poor, your huddled masses yearning to drive a new Cadillac."

"You got it. But tell me. What is it you want to do when you get through doing this?"

"Be a TV interviewer…"

"What'd you bring today, joker?"

"A little three cheese lasagna."

"Sounds good."

Just after lunch, Michael is summoned to JR's office,

"Michael, come into my office a sec, will ya?"

"Yes sir. What can I do for you?"

"My dad wants to meet you. Follow me."

Michael is taken around a bank of files, through a door, around a corner and into a part of the building he's never seen to meet a man who has, until now, been only a rumor. The office of Mr. H., into which he is now being ushered, is sumptuous. It reeks rich…with dark woods, leather armchairs, expansive mahogany desk and knick-knacks from antique stores. No garage sale merchandise here. But Michael notices only one framed picture, of a young dark skinned boy.

"Mr. Wade. I'm Bentley Harrison. Please, have a seat," which Michael does as JR leaves. The heavily southern accented; deep basso profundo voice of Mr. H is unsettling to Michael. He imagines that if a southern Baptist was blindfolded and heard this voice that the Baptist would assume he was being addressed by the Almighty. A person from another part of the world would probably doubt that God is from Georgia. Mr. H continues as he asks,

"Do you prefer Mike or Michael?"

"Always Michael, sir."

"Michael, you've been here a couple of weeks now and you haven't done shit. Do you like your work Michael?"

"Well, yes sir. (He lies) I'm just settling in; I never have done this kind of work before I came here."

"If you want to stay; you've got to produce. Are you familiar with the Cadillac diet?"

"No, sir."

"This is where we help our clientele shed a few pounds by separating them from their money. And the more weight they lose; the better. After all, we want our clients to be fit looking, now don't we?", he says not really looking for an answer. "Anyone that walks in here with a fat bulging wallet should walk out of here looking slimmer. I mean a fat wallet could even throw off a person's balance. It could even cause severe back problems. Now we can't have that, can we? Indeed, it's our duty to help these people walk taller and lighter. Do you know that studies prove that the closer a person spends to the sticker price of a car, the less likely they are to complain about that car later? It's psychological. If it's expensive; it must be good! Now, I want you to go out there and separate our money from these people. Your job depends on it!"

"Yes, sir."

As he exits, Michael tries to appear uplifted; as if what he had just heard is inspiring. In truth, he's thinking that now he knows why most of the long-time sales people here are jerks. What the hell was he thinking; him—a car salesman? He scanned the showroom; looking around at the various cubicles occupied with sales people working their dietetic scams on their customers. The really odd thing, he thought, is that these sales types don't even appreciate the people that spend money with them. After a sale, they'll go back to the dirty disgusting back room and brag about how they just shafted some poor asshole and how big their commission will be. He glances at Nicholas Santos, eagerly thrusting his face into that of his over-the-desk prospect, and realizes this guy has been here for twenty years. He's totally self-absorbed and he has an ex-wife that hates him. He gets his customers from the Greek community through the Greek Orthodox Church where he goes every Sunday and participates in all the festivals and fund-raisers and then belittles them all behind their backs. 'To whom could he be praying?', Michael wonders. His attention then swivels a couple of cubes over to George Suffian. Suffian is a pompous little bald-headed fart that walks on his tiptoes as if in high heels. His customers come from the Jewish community as well as several wealthy local families that all knew his dad. Suffian also has a surprising number of equally tiptoed customers. Speaking of farts. Bobinsky must have dropped another one. Michael discerns this as his attention is caught by the motion of her customers politely wriggling in her booth as they try to lift their noses above the level of the cubicle glass without actually resorting to holding their noses. What a way to sell cars!

"A.T., how are you? We don't see you often enough around here." Michael hears Vivian (the attractive forty-something blonde greeter) address a gorgeous thirtyish blonde woman entering the front door. He estimates she must be about the same height as Vivian as she is visible over the frosted glass partitions as is Vivian. That would make her about 5ft. 8 in.

"Fine, Vivian. I simply don't have enough time what with running the insurance business and taking care of Trey. (She speaks with a hint of tiredness but becomes brighter as she says) I think about y'all all the time. I miss you. JR in?"

"Yeah, go on back. You look great."

And she does look great. But she must have some sort of walking impediment as Michael regards her jerky, uneven motions as she points herself toward JR's office. As she rounds the cubular obstacle to Michael's vision; he realizes her movements are due to being dragged and pulled by a young dark-skinned boy.

"Come on Mom; let's see Grampa!"

It's the same boy that's in the framed photo in the office of Mr. H. This must be Mrs. H. III and she's being lead by the young Mr. H. IV. HIV, boy how'd you like those initials? Michael opines as he follows the twosome with his eyes.

"Let's go see Daddy, first. Alright Trey?"

The boy's frame becomes tighter and his pace slows. As they near JR's office the boy stops completely; his face downcast. JR comes out to greet them and goes first to the boy who almost wriggles out of his uneasy embrace.

"Hey, son. How are you?" JR's words are hesitant and sound less than heartfelt. They are certainly spoken with far less than his usual bluster. He also appears to be avoiding AT's attempts at kissing him hello. Mr. H must have been alerted to his Grandson's presence for he suddenly emerges from the H-cave with a large smile and hugs for both Grandson and daughter-in-law.

Michael notices a tall Black man, perhaps 6 ft.5 wearing a tan knit shirt and jeans, coming through the front door. Michael also sees no one moving toward the man. This is counter to the usual 'blood in the water' reaction of the sales force. He remembers Whitey's advice and asks Vivian whether he may wait on this gentleman.

"Sure. I don't see anyone else charging forward."

"Hi, sir, Michael Wade. How may I help you?"

A deep steadily measured voice responds,

"Hello. I'm looking for a used limo. I want to make two payments of $9,999.00 each. Got anything?"

"I think so. What's your name?"

"Monte St. James"

"Well, Mr. St…"

"Monte. Just call me Monte."

"Monte, I'll have to go ask the manager what he's willing to sell. He does keep a few classics to use for visiting bigwigs. Can you give me a minute to check with him?"

"Sure can." Michael begins to turn towards JR's office and turns back.

"May I ask you, will you be having a driver? That is, do you need a dividing screen between the front and back?"

"Yes, my bodyguard will be driving. And yes, definitely a privacy factor."

"Monte, I suppose some things are best left unsaid…but you must be 6 ft 5; why would *you* need a bodyguard."

"Somebody's got to tell me when to duck."

Michael nervously chuckles the surprise right off his face and thinks, "What is *this* deal? Not mine to reason why! He goes back to JR's office and sees that the blinds are drawn and the door is shut. He knocks firmly but gently.

"Just a minute." He hears JR say as a drawer slams shut.

"OK. Come in."

As he enters, he's surprised to see only JR,

"JR. there's a guy out here that wants a used limo. What should I show him?"

"How much does he have to spend?"

"About twenty grand."

"Show him the '89."

"What if he doesn't like the body style?"

"Try the '90…and if you have to, the '91."

"Numbers?"

"See what he likes first," JR sniffs and wipes his nose of a white residue.

"Was that your wife and kid earlier?"

"Yeah."

"Good looking family."

"Yeah."

'So much for that thought'…Michael thinks as he heads to grab three sets of keys from the key board near the switchboard and returns to his customer.

Mr. St…"

"Monte. Call me Monte."

"Monte, follow me", and Michael makes a sweeping overhand gesture as if leading a cavalry charge. They go out the front door, cross the street, go through the service department and out into a large back lot filled with all kinds of cars in everything from immaculate to decrepit condition. Monte's not too crazy about the '89 boat and prefers the sleeker lines of '90 or '91. Michael needs to know something about the unusual request regarding the payments,

"Why the two payments?"

"Let's just say...tax reasons."

"Monte, if you don't want to go over that twenty grand figure, you'd better take the '90 what with taxes, licenses, paperwork fees and all."

"OK. Wrap it up. I'll take it."

"Monte, I'll have to work it this way. Give us the first chunk now and we'll put this car out as a demo for a week and get that money processed. Then you come in next week and do the final paperwork, OK?"

"You got it, Mr. Wade."

"Michael. Call me Michael."

After the St. James paperwork is completed and Monte has embarked to, no doubt, pick up his bodyguard; Mr. H comes out to say,

"Michael Wade. Congratulations! That wasn't very hard, now, was it?"

"Not at all. Thank you." They walk out the side door together, Michael knows that it was, more acccurately, the advice of Mr. Grayer; but the owner is welcome to pat himself on the back. As they exit, a car in the distance can be heard loudly rumbling before it comes into view. As it nears and slowly pulls up to the dealership. Michael recognizes the rough looking late '80's de Ville as a vehicle belonging to a friend of Skates. Sure enough, Skates bounds out of the car and approaches his Dad. Skates has several scruffy looking companions in the midnight blue Caddy. Most of the kids look a notch below Skates with their scraggly goatees and vaguely criminal demeanor.

"Hey, Dad, can I use the car tonight?"

"Got a date?"

"Naw, I wanta go and see what's happening at the cross tonight."

"Oh, I'm sorry. This is the owner, Mr. Harrison-you've met his son, JR."

Michael makes introductory motions as Skates extends his hand. Michael is proud that his son can look anybody in the eye, in contrast to his buddies in the car—all looking slightly guilty about nothing in particular. Michael continues the intros with,

"Mr. H, my son, Skates."

"He does?"

"Yes, but…well…that's his name, too."

"Oh, I see. Hello, son. Your dad just made a sale!"

"Great Dad! Then, can I have some money, too?" he says grinning, under a suppressed laugh.

"Maybe. But what's the deal at the cross?"

"Everyone says the face of Jesus is appearing at night. There's a group there praying that think it's a sign he's coming back."

"Reminds me of that bumper sticker that says, 'Jesus is coming. Look busy…' ",Michael says with a half-smile that mirrors the sly grin of his offspring. They decide to meet at the house later and go check it out together.

As he drives home after work, Michael is feeling pretty good about his sale today. It was different, unexpected and interesting. He's appreciating this small victory when a red traffic light brings him to a halt. While waiting for the green, his eye is caught by the astonishing number of cars which have on their bumpers the Icthyus fish symbol that was used in ancient times for Christians to secretly identify each other. They seem everywhere around him. Well not everywhere, he decides, as he now sees an almost equal number of the Darwin symbol bumper stickers on vehicular backsides. The Darwin, or evolution, symbol is simply the Icthyus with legs or little feet protruding from the bottom as if the fish had emerged from the ocean onto land and…well evolved, adapted. The next bumper sticker he sees is of an Icthyus devouring a

Darwin symbol. They must be way far right', he thinks. There must be a real bumper sticker war going on here as he then sees one that says,

God, Please Save Me From Your Followers

This one gives him an internal twinge as he recalls all the carnage inflicted upon people, past, and present, in the name of God. This triggers a series of thoughts that include what really scares Christians about Muslims is that Muslims will tell you they're going to kill you in the name of God while Christians will tell you they love you and that murder is a sin while they kill you. He's learned that this town has a fairly large percentage of gays. The more visible of the two gay sexes here is the lesbian variety. A gay male friend in Miami told him that, in general, gay men prefer the raucous atmosphere of South Beach while gay women, in general, prefer a quieter laid back town like San Jacinto. Maybe San Francisco is an exception, he thinks. What causes these thoughts is that several of the Darwinian cars seem to be driven by women who, as Robin Williams once said, wear comfortable shoes. As the light changes, and the journey home continues, he nears his street and prepares to turn off the main drag. Before he does, he sees one final bumper sticker that best reflects his own point of view,

God is Too Big for One Religion

As a child, Michael had a loving Christian upbringing. His folks were Methodists, to be precise. He'd loved singing the Christian childrens songs like

'Jesus Loves me this I know
for the Bible tells me so
little ones to him belong
they are weak while He is strong...'
and
'Red and yellow black and white

they are precious in his sight
Jesus Loves the little children of the world.'

Those early experiences made him feel special, protected and Loved. He even used to have in his room a small paper picture of Jesus. It had instructions on the back that said to stare at the picture and then look away. If he stared long enough, when he looked away he could still see Jesus. It was slightly magical to him. He had had great parents that showed him their Love. He felt both lucky and grateful for that. That early knowledge of Love had often carried him through hard times. He was determined to ensure that his son would also always know that kind of Love. As Michael had grown, he noticed strange uses for religion occurring that caused him to delve deeper into the mysteries of life and Love and Spirit. He noticed so many people using religion and Jesus to obtain power, position, wealth and even to wage war. 'Thou shalt not what?', he thought. He remembered coming across a book when he was quite young about the great religions of the world. It showed many religious rituals and explained basic beliefs. What he most enjoyed were the pictures of the people. People from all over the world. All in search of and praising the divine in their own way. It was particularly interesting because, back then; there wasn't much diversity in his corner of America. His America was overwhelmingly white and waspy with a few Catholics and a couple of Jews. There were some Blacks in a background capacity. There were a few Chinese down at the Ming Palace Restaurant. It was fair to say that he knew as many Jews as Chinese. And that was it. His child's America was very small.

He had vivid nighttime dreams then. One that re-occurred often he knew to be his life before the present. This was odd, as he'd never heard of re-incarnation. He told no one. It wasn't a nightmare. It felt like a message. He dreamed he was a young man running across a battlefield. He was dressed as a soldier with a metal helmet that had a pointed spike on top and he held a rifle. As he ran in the dream, there were explosions all around and then he was blown up and vaporized into the sky. It didn't scare him, it wasn't painful and it brought on no painful memories. It seemed like a fact. Many years hence he was told by a psychic he respected, and whom he had never told about the dream, that the Akashic records held that Michael had been a seventeen year old German conscript in World War I and had died in battle. Maybe that's why he detested violence and war in this life.

Another influential childhood recollection was of coming across a picture in Life Magazine of a little boy about Michael's age at that time. The boy was from some African country he could no longer recall. He was sure the country had a different name by now anyway. The boy had been caught up in some 'adult' war being waged around him and a leg had been blown off. In the picture the boy was standing on crutches and had his stump of a leg wrapped with bandages. What had struck Michael's heart was that the boy had this huge, happy, grateful grin. He was so happy to be alive. Michael carried that picture in his wallet well into adulthood. On the picture he had scribbled 'that giant within you is a small part of God.' Whenever he felt down he would pull out this picture and mutter a silent prayer of thanks that his troubles were so tiny in comparison. To him, giving thanks had become the purest form of prayer.

Michael parks and enters his home and finds Skates in the living room and hugs him hello and asks if he's ready to check out the church. He is and they jump back into the Hyundai and begin to head toward the tall cross. Twilight isn't far away and the cross, being on the eastern edge of this east coast town, will be one of the last things visible to the townspeople to reflect the sun's glory, due to its height.

In this current period, there sits a modern Catholic church to the right of the cross and a large expanse of green surrounding. Directly in front of the cross, on the landward side, is a man-made reflecting pond with a wide footbridge leading from the area of the church over the pond to a smaller green space directly under and around the cross before the land ends completely and the Bay of Serapis begins. To the left of the cross, looking from the street is a variety of buildings and small structures. This area is reached either by crossing the footbridge and turning left or by walking left across the open green and past a few olive trees and smaller shrubs. Nearest to the cross and closest to the water is a very old graveyard with green algae covered tombstones with Spanish names inscribed thereon. In the middle of the graveyard is a quaint stone chapel. Inside is a wooden altar with pictures of saints and Mary and many flickering votive offerings. This area is well shaded with old oaks and some palm trees and feels quite peaceful. Still further left are newer buildings. The most prevalent are the gift shop and the church offices. Less obvious and just across the street from the church offices, is the group of houses that are occupied by the priest and others of the church hierarchy. The entire site is called the Church of Nuestra Senora de la Leche Perpetuo.

"Dad, the peacefulness here is amazing...especially when you know how much blood has been spilled on this ground," Skates says surveying the serenity of the site.

"Yeah, pretty amazing. The destruction of an entire race of people began right here."

"Except for those that made it into the Everglades."

"And those weren't even the original Native Americans. That was three hundred years later. The first people here were wiped out."

Not only that, but there had been invasions of the Spanish by the French and English. Pirates had menaced the town. Twice it had been burnt to the ground.

Slave ships had traded here. Civil war skirmishes had taken place in the area. Much misery had occurred in this currently contented spot.

As Michael and Skates leave the parking area and begin walking toward the cross they notice that the crowd near its base has grown to about three-dozen. Two figures stand out from and away from the group near the church entrance. They are a traditionally garbed priest and nun. Michael decides to approach them. The priest looks about thirty years old and is slenderly built, average height, with short dark hair. The nun is shorter than the priest and has a sparkling freckled face. Michael imagines red hair underneath the hood of her habit. They both have something in common-truly genuine appearing smiles—as Michael and son approach. Michael ascertains, as he introduces his son and himself, that the priest is Father Leonard (or Lenny, as he prefers) and the nun is Sister Grace. After some small talk Michael asks,

"What's going on here, do you know?

Father Lenny replies,

"A short time ago, a homeless man named Jesse Rod claimed that he saw the face of Jesus appear above the cross. He told someone who told someone else and word started getting around. I personally haven't seen any such as he claims. But people have begun to gather to wait and watch. Some of them are of my flock; some are homeless, some just curious." Michael peruses those gathered and wonders at the accuracy of Lenny's description. None of them looks homeless, although one looks somewhat scraggy. And most of them look like snowbirds. People from somewhere else; although it's the wrong time of year for their migration. "But each sundown a few more people seem to show up. I'm sure they're expecting something miraculous to occur. I just hope the faithful remain faithful even if they are temporarily disappointed. People too often place their faith in signs and wonders instead of the innate knowledge of their hearts."

At that moment a collective gasp rises from the crowd and the four turn to see all eyes riveted to the top of the cross. A large luminous white cloud seems to hover just behind the tall gleaming cross as the earth rotates so that the day's final rays of sun strike the center of the cross bar sending out a blinding glint of sun on metal. Then the cloud seems to evenly divide into a darkened half, as if to rain, and the other half remains a pure ivory white. It's the summer solstice and the sky is halved into black and white. As the sun recedes, night quickly descends and people stand as if struck dumb.

Murmurings begin to be heard from the crowd. What had they seen? One voice is heard to say,

"I saw the face of Christ in the clouds!"

Another says,

"He is coming! He is risen!"

"Judgement is near!"

Off to the side Michael, Skates, Lenny and Grace are still staring at the top of the now darkened cross. Skates excitedly says,

"Dad, did you see that? It was beautiful! WOW!"

"Yeah, truly gorgeous. Did any of you see a face in the clouds?"

All those he is addressing signify,

"No."

The crowds' fringes begins to peel off and leave the area. Many appear to be still dazed. A core group of a dozen is left near the base and they begin to re-kindle the fire that Michael had seen the other night. Michael asks Father Leonard and Sister Grace if any of the twelve are their parishioners. Lenny says,

"No, I only recognize one of them and that's Jesse Rod; the man who first reported seeing the vision."

"Which one is he?"

"That average looking fortyish fellow with the scruffy gray beard. His clothes seem to have improved since I first saw him."

Skates bursts into the conversation with,

"Father...I mean Dad-sorry Father Leonard-that guy used to hang around downtown bothering the tourists for money. He used to hassle us skaters, too. We thought he was...well, a little nuts...and a little dangerous. He looks so calm now.He didn't used to be this way."

Father Leonard says,

"If this gets around more than it has already, we'll be having a lot more tourists in town. Do you remember the windowpane in Tampa that was said to have the image of Christ embedded in it? Thousands came to look everyday for weeks. I think the building manager finally had the panel painted...or removed."

Michael wants to know,

"Father, what does the church do in cases like this?" "Well, should more solid evidence occur than I've seen to date; they would send someone to investigate. In the meantime, I don't mind these people staying here and praying. If it brings just one person to Christ and the church, I'll be happy."

Grace interjects,

"Lenny, uh...I mean Father Leonard, we'd best be going now."

"Yes Grace, you're right. Michael, Skates-very good to meet you. Please drop by anytime."

Grace and Lenny leave heading toward the complex of buildings to the left of the cross. Skates says,

"Dad, let's go talk to those people."

"OK," and they saunter over and are spotted by Jesse Rod who seems to recognize Skates. Jesse begins running toward them, which causes Skates to re-coil, as he's unsure of Jesse's motivation. As Jesse reaches them, he says,

"Son, I'm sorry. I know I was mean to you and your friends. My head wasn't right.

I'm sorry. Now, I'm saved; washed in the blood of the lamb."

Skates looks shocked at the words of Jesse Rod. He can't deny that Rod does seem changed. He asks,

"What happened to change you?"

"I was walking by here a couple of weeks ago in my usual state... around sundown. I looked up at the cross and was blinded by a flash of light...and then...I saw it...the face of Jesus...in the clouds behind the cross. I started to weep. I fell down on my knees and I just wailed...cried and cried. I thought about how good I was as a boy and my folks and being raised in the church and how far I'd drifted away from everything

I used to know. I didn't know what to do. So...I just kept on walking. But, I had this gnawing pain inside...this feeling that I had to change. I just kept walking until I came to the appliance store on Main. They had this huge big screen TV on in the window. Reverend T.G. Baker was on. You know him?'

Skates and Michael shake their heads no as Jesse continues,

"He's that TV preacher out of Lordstown, Ohio...got a national show every night. He's got that big blonde hair...like a lions mane ...Christian."

Michael's thinking, 'wait a minute...I have seen that guy while channel surfing through the six billion useless satellite offerings. He's one of those holy-rollier than thou TV give me your money preachers. His wife's got her wigs of many colors to accent her poor taste in clothes'... Jesse continues the recounting of his salvation, "I could just barely hear the sound through the store window but I heard him say something about if you've seen Jesus-you've been saved. I ran to the nearest pay phone and called their 800# and told 'em my story. Rev. Baker took my call right there...live...on the air. He said, 'Don't despair, son. You've been blessed! I'll send some of my flock to watch over you.' And he did. These people showed up a couple of days later, gave me clothes...and a place to sleep...and...they made me feel 'found' again. Praise the Lord! Would you like to meet some of the reverend's people?"

"Well, I wouldn't mind just saying howdy..." as they are introduced around, Michael would like to ask if they saw the image of Christ today; because he didn't. And neither did Skates, the Father or Sister Grace. But he doesn't want to get involved in a religious discussion with these folks. It has been his experience that there are few things as scary as angry theologians. But Skates, being younger and less concerned with people's perception of him, blurts out,

"Did any of you see Jesus?...here...today?" a woman named Esther replies,

"Of course! Didn't you?"

"No, ma'am."

"You must be a heathen. (The way her tongue strikes her front teeth on the 'th' in heathen reminds Skates of a serpent's tongue.) Jesus only appears to the true believer." Esther states to Skates as he mumbles under his breath,

"Or to the truly deluded…". Michael decides to end the potential hostility by saying, "Uh…son, why don't we have this discussion some other time? Listen folks, I hope you enjoy your stay here. Here's my card. Please call on me if you feel I could help you in any way."

As they head back to the car, Michael is momentarily embarrassed and then discards that emotion for pride in his son who only asked an honest question and spoke the truth.

As they reach the trusty Hyundai, Michael sees a small white Plymouth pulling onto San Jacinto Boulevard from the area of the church offices. He swears it looks like Father Leonard driving. Only there's some redheaded woman sitting very close to him. He involuntarily utters one of his made-up expressions,

"Well, Butras Butras Golly…"

"What, Dad?"

"Nothing son. Nothing."

White Turkey Chili with Salsa Verde

❀

In a large pan, combine and cook ¾ lb. ground turkey, ½ cup chopped onion and 1 minced garlic clove. Stir in 3 cups water, 15 oz. can of white beans, 4 oz. canned diced green chili peppers, 2 tsps. bouillon granules, 1 tsp. cumin powder and ¼ tsp. ground white pepper. Bring to boil, cover, reduce heat and simmer for 30 minutes.

In separate small bowl make a roux by mixing ¼ cup hot water and 2 tbsp. flour.

Add roux to turkey mix, cook and sir 'til thick and bubbly. Continue cooking and stirring one minute more.

Top each serving with shredded white cheese and salsa verde.

Salsa Verde

In medium mixing bowl, put 5-6 chopped tomatillos (husk removed) *or* one 13 oz. can drained and chopped tomatillos with 2 tbsp. chopped onion, 2 hot (but seeded) peppers, 1 tbsp. cilantro powder (or several fresh shredded leaves) 1 tsp. shredded lime peel and ½ tsp. honey. Cover and refrigerate 'til needed.

CHAPTER THREE

Thank God!

A couple of days later, Michael is sitting at his desk at the Cadillac shop when he is paged over the P.A. that there is a call for him. As he answers, an unfamiliar voice asks,

"Hello, is that Mr. Wade?

"Yes."

"My name is Tom Jude. I was in Rev. Baker's group at the cross the other night. You gave me your card." Michael is surprised, but grateful, to hear from one of these folks.

"Yes, sir. How may I help you?'

"Well, first of all…I'd like to ask your co-operation in keeping what I'm about to tell you as confidential as possible. May I have your word on that?"

"Of course you can…within the bounds of the law and so on…you understand.

Why don't you tell me a little more about what it is that you need?"

"Certainly. Reverend Baker has decided to visit San Jacinto and, perhaps, hold a revival here…maybe even do a few broadcasts from here. First, let me ask you, have you been born again?"

"Well, I think that's between the Lord and me. Why do you ask?"

"Rev. Baker only likes to do business with people of like mind, know what I mean?" Michael doesn't want to lie, but he really needs the business. Whatever that may be. He mentally rationalizes that we've all been born again. Perhaps hundreds of times, if you accept re-incarnation. And Michael does. So…even though he knows it's not precisely what Mr. Jude means, he responds,

"Yes, I have been born again." He silently thinks 'and, Lord knows, I've been *saved* a thousand times, too. Thank God…is that what the reverend's initials stand for? TG, Thank God Baker? Pompous, pompadoured putz!'

"Good, Mr. Wade. Now here's what the Reverend has asked me to procure. He needs three limousines to use for his stay here…he'll supply his own drivers. Can you handle that for us?"

"Yes, sir!", he says, barely able to control his enthusiasm.

"Mr. Jude, tell me the where and when and I'll take care of everything else for you."

Jude relates the particulars and Michael hangs up. He almost let's out a whoop; but decides to defer to the false decorum of the establishment and goes to the smoking area out back to share his glee with the other sales people.

JR, Nero and Nick Santos are there. Michael, grinning from ear to ear, says,

"Got another one. A guy wants to rent three limos for at least a month; maybe longer. How's that sound?" JR is the first to respond,

"Great man. Congratulations. How'd you do it?"

"Let's just call it a church connection." Nero Fox adds,

"Whatever works. Say, speaking of church, do ya want to join us for some golf (Michael thinks it humorous that a lot of southerners pronounce golf as 'goff', which Nero does.) on Sunday?"

"That's really nice of you, sir; but I try to spend some time with my son on Sundays. Besides, wasn't it St. Andrew who said, 'Golf is a good walk spoiled'?"

JR says,

"You could ask your son to come along. He seems like a nice kid. Of course, afterwards, we usually go to the topless joint out on 95."

Michael doesn't want to,outright, say no to his bosses, but he could care less about golf. He's only played a few times since the age of twelve when he quit golf after coming in second in a tournament. These guys even watch 'goff' on television. To him this is a supreme weirdness. The closest thing JR and Nero have to a religion is 'goff'…and football. Either the 'Gators or FSU *and* the Jaguars. Michael likes football; but will not die if deprived. These guys might.

"Let me ask Skates. He likes golf…and I'm pretty sure he likes breasts. I can let you know tomorrow. Thanks for asking." Nero Fox declares,

"You know, you could get pretty good at this. Go out and knock 'em dead."

Sub 3-1
Hyena

At the end of the day Michael drives home from work thinking, 'Jesus, is this what I really want to do?' Of course he already knows the answer is no. This is just a stopgap measure and it isn't working all that great. He's lied to a client. Albeit, one who'd asked him a rather personal question. It was none of Jude's business, but he'd lied. Beyond the normal civil constructs of society that preclude one from being unnecessarily rude to someone's face; he believes in being honest. More accurately, he believes in telling the truth to those who are able to accept it. Otherwise, it's pearls before swine. He can be very diplomatic. He didn't like making people feel bad unless they really needed it. Then this frightening thought flies through his head. 'Am I becoming like them-the salesmen?'

Something's got to change. Michael also feels his chronological clock ticking away. He's very lonely for someone to Love. Sundays with Skates are important to him. But Skates is at the age where Michael feels that his son is just being nice to him by hanging with him on Sundays. It's just a matter of time before Skates gets serious with his new found girl or decides to hit the road to a more adventurous locale. And the nights…the nights are so very long and lonely. Where the heck is Michael Wade going to meet someone? Here he is; the new guy on the block in a very tiny town, he barely has a job, very small cash flow and he's living with his teenage son. Plus, he's older than he's ever been and his marital track record leaves a discerning woman with a lot to consider. But, hey…Ted Bundy had women begging to marry him while he was on death row. Maybe he's got a shot!

As Michael tools his car past Our Lady of Perpetual Leche he gazes toward the imposing cross to see that, now, there are perhaps fifty people encamped at its base. Word is getting around. And he's heading home…

As Michael steps through his back door and into the kitchen, he sees a note,

> Dad,
> I went out for a while.
> See you later.
> Love, Skates

Suddenly, images of barbeque and blues dance in his head and he slips into the more casual attire of shorts and tank top. The sultry summer day is giving way to the more tender time of twilight. Michael decides to stretch his legs by walking out into the night to Mother Marys. He doesn't think it's any big deal to walk around Washington Heights after dark even though others of like complexion have warned him not to do so. But he's been in more deadly locales than this and puts one foot after the other. He turns up Abbeyville Road past the peeling painted shops of the once thriving Black business district. Integration hadn't treated this area any better than it had Overtown in Miami or Sweet Auburn in Atlanta. There are still beautiful churches in the 'Heights' that often yield the magnificent singing of powerful voices lifted in praise. But not tonight. It's just quiet. Ominously quiet. Dark figures dart in and out of doorways while doing deals in dark clothing made darker still by the absence of light; save for a few sporadically placed street lights. Many of which have been strategically darkened to disguise the dispensation of certain controlled substances. Michael realizes, 'the only thing I like about the dark-is the light'. As the rib shack comes into view; Michael is relieved to see the peaceful, inviting lights and swaying palms. The joint is jumping. Whitey's on stage singing Nappy Brown's version of 'The Nighttime is the Right Time' and the place is packed. Michael's already sweating from the walk so he wipes his brow as he enters the din. Mary's behind the bar still poised and coiffed even with all the activity swirling around her. He has to shout to her across the bar to be heard,

"Yo, Mary. How are you?"

"Lordy, what'd you do, walk here? Here use this towel to get some of that perspiration off of you."

"Thanks. How 'bout a Red Stripe?"

"What's that…Red Stripe?"

"Please."

"Here you go. You be careful out there walking around at night; you hear?"

"Yes, ma'am."

"What's that news truck doing outside?"

"New truck? We didn't get any new truck."

"No, a news truck. Like from a TV station or something. It's got a satellite dish on top."

"It must belong to that couple over there. They're about the only people in here I don't know."

Michael turns to see an extremely attractive…well…a White woman. She's probably between thirty and thirty-five with dark brown curly hair just below shoulder length. She has a pretty smile and warm brown eyes. She's laughing with her tablemate. He's a Black man in his thirties, he guesses. He's kind of good looking too; but of far less interest to Michael's hormones. His eyes return to the brown-eyed woman. Great visuals; but she appears to be taken. Mary Rose motions for him to move to the far end of the bar so that they may better converse.

"So, you don't know who they are?"

"No…came in an hour or so ago, sat down and ordered some food. They seem to be having a good time but it doesn't seem they know anyone here. What'll you have tonight?"

"Miz Mary Rose, I think I'm just going to have a couple of beers tonight and go home. I just had to be someplace 'real' for a while. Say…how does Whitey handle it at Cadillac year after year?"

"Well, Michael…I think he's pretty happy overall and that helps no matter what else life brings you. You not too happy over there?"

"Nah…just worried I'll become like the rest of them."

"Nope. Won't happen. I can tell. You're different. I think you actually care."

"I do. But it's like long term exposure to low doses of radiation Gradually it can take its toll."

"You know that you're the only one from Cadillac to ever set foot in here."

"Strange…it's a great place. Not even Charles or Jones?"

"Nope. Not once."

Whitey announces a break and the jukebox takes over the musical duties of the house as he moves to greet Michael,

"Hey, how you doing? How's things going?"

"OK. Nice work up there. You sound great."

"Thanks, man. I enjoy it."

"Say the other day I saw a woman…I think it's JR's wife…come into the showroom. Her name was 'AT? Something like that."

"Agnus Tarragon Carmen; now AT Harrison. Incredible woman. She used to date another man at Cadillac…Richard Black. Then JR and her started going out."

"He seemed so cold to her…and his kid…I guess it must have been his kid. The kid shied away from him but ran to Mr. H…"

"It's not an unusual thing for kids to be closer to their grandparents and I don't think JR's ever been certain his kid is his. That's also why he's cold to AT."

"That kid doesn't resemble any Harrison I've met."

"No, I think JR suspects it may be Richards."

"Black?"

"Yeah. He is Black. But I've known AT for years and she's no cheater …honorable hard working woman from a hard working family. I think it's just some odd genetic thing. You know she's got her own insurance agency…"

"Oh, yeah…"

"Yeah, that's how she got involved with all the car guys…drumming up business."

"What ever happened to Black?"

"He got sent up for some fraud deal. I never was too clear on what happened. Something to do with some missing money from Cadillac. He should be out in a couple of years."

"Was that why she stopped dating him?"

"No. That was after AT and JR got married. After the baby was born."

"Things that make you go 'hmmm'."

"No, I don't think so. He was a pretty shifty dude. Listen, I'm going to get up there again…you going to hang around?"

"No Whitey, I'm going to walk on home."

"You walked here? Be careful out there, man."

"Thanks. See you at work. Bye Mary."

Michael slowly ambles down Abbeyville Road towards home. He's in a reflective, contemplative mood…kind of on autopilot. He pays the shadowy figures scant attention; forgetting to use body language to keep those that prey on others at bay. As he rounds a corner he notices a young fellow on a bicycle pass by. Michael nods and says a muffled hello. Under the next darkened street lamp, the same boy appears and jumps off his bike and throws it to the ground. He swiftly and threateningly accosts Michael,

"Give me all your money or I'll kill you!"

Michael's reverie is shattered. What's going on…this is his neighborhood, too. Instinctively, he begins backing away from his attacker but can see no direct way out of this. Despite his large build; he ain't no fighter.

"Come on man. I live here." He says thinking the kid must be mistaking him for some cracker lookin' for crack in the 'Black' part of town and he keeps backing up. "Give me your money or I'll shoot you!" Michael knows he should comply, but this really pisses him off. He has a habit of carrying his money in two different pockets; mainly for pickpockets. He's not carrying that much, but he doesn't have that much anywhere. He's got a twenty in one pocket and forty bucks in the other. He proffers the twenty, figuring this much isn't worth dying for,

"Take it, man. But you're fuckin' up."

Just as he hands the kid the twenty he hears the sound of an oncoming vehicle. Suddenly the scene is bathed in bright white light. Michael can't see the light's source but for the first time he can make out the kid's features and what looks like a gun barrel extending from the kid's hand. The kid decides to bolt; but not before bringing the gleaming metal up alongside Michael's head as he momentarily fades to black.

In a couple of minutes, Michael's shaking off the blow as he finds himself sitting on the curb. Above him is the attractive Black and White couple from the rib joint. The man is shouldering a large TV camera with its lights now dimmed. The woman says,

"You OK?"

"Yeah…I think so. Am I bleeding?"

The man says,

"No, But you're going to have a heck of a bruise there. What happened?"

"Oh…I was just walking home and this kid jumped me. For twenty bucks. Chickenshit little fart." The man wants to know,

"Were you trying to score? The kid was yelling 'You do creck' as he ran away."

"Creck, what the hell is that?"

"The urban pronunciation of crack."

"I was just up at Mother Mary's Ribs. I saw you all there. I just live a block away from here. I wasn't trying to score…just walking home."

"Yeah, we saw you at the bar. You and Mary Diana kind of stood out up there."

"I guess that kid thought I stood out a little bit, too. (Michael rubs his head) Damn, it pisses me off. One more block and I'd been home …Shit. Sorry, I don't mean to curse. Mary Diana…that your name? (He offers a hand) Michael Wade (to the gentleman) Hi, Michael Wade."

"Moses Abraham."

"Thanks, you all. I appreciate it." Moses tries to help Michael from the curb. He's a tad wobbly. Mary Diana offers,

"Look, should we call the police for you or can we take you home?"

"Maybe, just take me home, please." His rescuers help him into the van and cart him the short distance to his place.

"Would you come in for a minute?'

"Sure", they reply. Mary Diana is immediately struck by how cute the cottage is. She thinks it's kind of a tropical Cape Cod style with the little wooden gate and the welcoming allure of the trees and flowers. As they enter the back door and go through the countryish kitchen she senses that there must be a woman around. It's just too neat and charming for a single man. They continue on through the breakfast nook into a formal dining area with beautiful antique furnishings that then leads into a large living room with a fireplace, comfy sofas and a large bay window looking out onto…a lake?

"Skates, you here, man?" Michael calls out to no reply.

"My son, Skates…"

"He does?"

"Well…yes; but that's his name, too. I guess he's out. Just as well. I'd like to collect myself a bit so I don't freak him out."

"How old's your son?', Mary Diana wants to know.

"Eighteen. Good kid. I Love him."

"This place is a lot bigger than it looks from the outside. And your furniture…it's gorgeous. Is that a lake out there?"

"Thanks, Yeah, we were lucky to have found this place. It's peaceful. You want to see the lake? Step this way." Michael's starting to feel better now and he's glad for the company. He leads them to the 'front' door that opens onto a small but lovely lagoon.

"According to old records that I've seen, there used to be a narrow street that ran along this side of the house. So, all of the main entrances of the lakeside homes face the lake; even though people now come into their homes through the (here he shapes the first two fingers on each hand as if framing an invisible word hung in the air in front of him) quote-unquote 'back' door."

Moses says,

"Did you know that social scientists say this is the sort of locale that we all look for? They've determined that early humans felt safest near a source of water that was protected and from where they could look out…and see…in all directions to make sure nothing was gaining on them."

"No kidding. Well, now I know why I like it here so much. You guys never did mention why you're here in town. Y'all from Jacksonville?"

"Moses is. I'm based in LA. I guess you don't recognize me."

"I'm sorry, no, I don't. Where should I know you from?"

"20-20. I do a segment called MD's 20-20. It's about interesting topics people may not otherwise hear about. I heard about the rumors here…about the giant cross…and people seeing visions of Christ…and now, we find out ol' TG Baker is coming down here. Thought there might be a story."

"Actually, I was there the other day at sundown and saw a really beautiful spectacle; but no Jesus. I don't know…maybe he only appears to those who believe hard enough…"

"Or to those who want to see him hard enough", Mary Diana completes Michael's thought as he continues,

"You know, I got a call from one of the reverends people. I work at the Cadillac place here. They want three limos for an unspecified period. I guess he plans on being here for a while once he arrives."

"When is he arriving? Do you know?"

"He'll be here in just a couple of days...coming in by private bus ...like a rock and roll tour."

"Michael, I'm going to need some transportation while I'm here as well. Can you hook me up?"

"Sure. What do you want?"

"I've always had an affinity for some of the older model Caddy cruisers...a convertible. If it's the right deal, I could even buy it and drive it back to LA."

"Sounds great. Why don't I pick something out for you...then I'll call you to come take a look."

"We're at the Casa Maria downtown."

"Mary, we should be going..."

"You're right, Mose. Michael, glad we could help."

"Me too. You guys may have been literal life savers. Thanks. Thank you very much."

Michael leads them out the 'back front' door. As Mary Diana and Mose reach the gate, he calls out,

"Hey, what's your room number?'

"316"

Sub 3-2
Coming to Agrippa

The next day Michael is on the phone at the dealership,

"316, please."

The phone answers in Mary's room; it's Moses,

"Moses, it's Michael, the guy you rescued last night..."

"Michael, how's your head today?"

"A little swelling; but not bad. I just feel stupid. I usually pay more attention to things than to let myself get into that kind of situation. I try to pay attention to the 'inner guide.' Listen, I had an idea…is Mary available?"

"Sure. Hang on. I'll get her for you."

Michael still can't tell what the relationship is between Moses and Mary. Is it professional? Or is it more? He's curious to find out.

"Hi Michael. Mary here. How are you today?"

"Pretty good…thanks to you. Listen, I have an idea. How'd you like to pick out your car and meet TG Baker at the same time?"

"Sounds good so far. What do you have in mind?"

"Well, I just heard from his people and they say his entourage will be here tomorrow at 3PM…and I think I've found a car for you. It's sleek and slick. An '87 El Dorado…only 60,000 miles. Red with a white top and red leather interior. I know this sounds just like a car guy; which I'm not, but I will give you the best possible price."

"It sounds beautimous. And that *does* sound like a car guy. Just don't screw me, OK?"

"It will be the best deal they'll let me give you. See you tomorrow at three."

As he signs off, he picks up a copy of the San Jacinto Light. The headline reads,

MIRACLE IN SAN JACINTO?

Underneath is a picture of the cross at sunset with the same glint of sun on metal that he witnessed. Still no image of Jesus; also like he witnessed. Below the photo is an account of the story to date. 'Only a few people claim to have actually seen the alleged image. They are mostly followers of TV evangelist TG Baker…"etc. etc…He takes the paper to show to JR,

"JR, you seen this?"

"No, I always turn straight to our ad in the classifieds. What's it say?"

JR peruses the article quickly,

"So…just a bunch of yahoos who've got nothin' better to see."

"No. The point is that this Rev. Baker is the guy who's getting three limos from us tomorrow."

"No shit? The guy from Ohio? Hold on, let me call dad", he punches up the intercom,

"Hey, dad. Did you read the paper today? No…no…there's nothing wrong with our ad. The front-page…yeah…the 'miracle'…right. Well, that's the guy Michael's got coming in tomorrow. No, not Jesus. TG Baker. Yeah, right away dad", he turns to Michael,

"Get in there. He wants to talk to you."

Michael obeys (like there's a choice) and follows the circuitous route back to the plush office of Mr. H.. He is there with a beautiful statuesque blonde woman who appears to be in her 50's.

"Michael Wade. I'd like you to meet my wife, Bernice. Honey, this is Michael…one of our new salesman. He's starting to make some contacts around town"; Bernice shakes Michael's hand in a practiced, warm manner. Whether or not she's sincere; he can't tell. But she sure is good at it.

"Michael, did you know that my wife's family built that cross that's on the front page? At least, their money did."

"No, sir. I didn't. I'm still learning a lot about the more recent history of San Jacinto."

"My wife would like to speak to you about that preacher coming here tomorrow." Michael hears a disturbing similarity in the voice of Mrs. H. and Mr. H. Hers is a feminine version of her husband's forceful southern drawl,

"Now Michael. My family's been here a long time. Like a lot of folks here in town, we're from the coastal regions of southern Italy. Long time gone, of course. My family name is Agrippa. You may have seen it around town (indeed he has; on the dry cleaners, the elementary school-well, it was all over.) That church is very special to us, and the cross is even more special. We don't want anything going on there to denigrate the site or it's reputation. How do you know this Rev. Baker?"

"Well, I don't, ma'am. I've seen him on TV…and I happened to meet some of his followers at the church the other night."

"Are you one of his followers?"

"No, ma'am. Just trying to make a living by selling to the few remaining souls in town that don't already do business with your husband's company."

"Michael, you should also know that I am vice-president of this company. When Mr. Baker arrives, I want you to make sure that my husband meets him, OK? We'd like to ascertain his motives."

"Yes, ma'am. Certainly."

As he's dismissed, he thinks, 'what a strange exchange; control freaks. Don't want anything going on without their knowing about it. They must have their fingers in a lot of pies. Speaking of pies; it's lunch time…'

Michael heads for the big oak out back and there sits Whitey.

"Good day, Michael. How'd you like the music last night?"

"Great. But I had a ringing in my head later that wasn't so melodic…" and he recounts the incident of the hold-up and subsequent rescue by the bright white news truck madonna saviour.

"You got whacked? Who did it? What'd they look like?"

"A light skinned, dark complected youth…"

"You mean he was black…"

"Yeah, I just hate such terms. Anyway, he was a skinny kid, late teens. He had on a black baseball cap with a white 'S' on it, baggy shirt, low slung jeans…maybe 5 foot 9…it was pretty dark 'til that news truck shined it's ever-lovin' light on me. I did notice that his bike had white-wall tires and the front one had a quarter sized red mark on it. And…oh yeah, a tiny gun that matched the size of his d…IQ."

"Right off, I can't think of who that is; but he must be from the 'Heights'. I'll put the word out."

"The money wasn't large, it just pisses me off that I was *one block* from my house; you know?"

"Ticks me off that someone's knocking off people leaving *my place*. I'll see what I can find out. What was the deal with those news people? You know; they were in the 'Station'...say, that girl was pretty..."

"She is pretty. She's getting a car from me tomorrow...but I can't figure out if she and the cameraman have a thing going..."

"I don't think so. Not if she's from LA. The cameraman's from Jax, channel 11. He's been down here before, shooting news stories and some commercials. He did the camera work on that one Mr. H. has running now."

"Cool. Maybe I've got a shot. Hey Whitey, what's the deal with Mrs. H...and their place in the community?" "Why'd she bring that up?"

"Oh, that Rev. Baker is about to become my customer tomorrow...and she seemed nervous about him being connected to 'her' cross."

"I wouldn't worry about it. More than likely they just want to figure out a way to make some money off him while he's in town..." Whitey says to his own amusement and then continues, "Mr. and Mrs. H, or her family, have something to do with just about anything that goes on in this town. You know, a few years ago, they found a load of coke in a car being transported up north...JR was driving. But everyone knows it was just 'family' business. Once JR got back to this jurisdiction; it all just kind of...faded away."

"Him, I had no idea; though I did once see a whitish powder creeping out of JR's nose."

"What you got today?" Whitey asks, returning to more everyday matters.

"A steak sandwich and caesar salad combo; you?"

"Smoked turkey and collards on the side."

Michael is worried about upsetting his current 'owners' and decides to call Mary Diana to ask her to be discreet when she comes to the dealership tomorrow,

"Mary, hi. Michael Wade here. Listen, there are a couple of things I'd like to tell you before we meet tomorrow…", in mid-sentence he makes a decision to test the waters,

"Right down from your hotel is a great place that we could meet so that I can give you this information. It's the Valencia Brew House. It overlooks the intra-coastal there. Could we meet there about 5:30?"

"Are you sure this isn't a date?"

"Well…it wasn't when I picked up the phone, but it may be by now. What do you say?"

"Well, OK. I'll see you there at 5:30."

At 5:29; Michael is at the Brew House. Mary's already there, standing near the curved dark wood downstairs bar.

"Hi, Mary! Did you order anything yet?"

"No, I just got here."

"Then how about we go upstairs and sit on the deck outside and catch some sea breeze? Actually, we could drink a couple, too."

She grins and accompanies him upstairs. The Brew House is a modern effort at looking old. It *is* an old building. It's been newly refurbished to emulate an early 1900's look. There's lots of exposed brick; probably authentic. They ascend a polished blonde wood staircase with brass handrails that leads upstairs to an even larger, and busier, dining area. Here there is also another bar and walls of still more exposed red brick. Clever planning gives every table a view of the outside. Pretty cool. And not pretentious. The owners have created an elegant setting without being stuffy. There are lots of energetic, slightly overly friendly wait staffers. You know the kind. They'll tell you their name without asking yours. This is Michael's favorite downtown hangout whenever he feels he can afford it. And besides, Skates busses tables here.

They are led by the hostess to a table on the wraparound deck. The deck has a panoramic view of the heart of the old city on one side and the city's harbor on the other. They select a table at the apex of the two corners. The best of all possible worlds, Michael muses. He's with a pretty woman in one of his favorite places.

From their vantage point, they can see the ancient town square that's borne witness to much history...and the bay with sailing boats gliding along underneath the graceful bridge built many decades ago. The scene is especially beautiful as, what photographers call, 'the Golden Hour' approaches. Towards the end of the day when the sun achieves a low western angle, views are enhanced as the brightest, most vivid light of the day bathes the bay. This is the sort of brilliance that abounds in southern California and caused film makers to abandon north Florida for the other coast in the early 1900's. The deck, upon which they sit, has white tables alongside a decorative, whitewashed cast iron railing interspersed with columns. Accenting the spaces between are hanging plants.

"You know...when I asked you here...I...I didn't even know I was going to ask you here...", he says with a nervous chuckle.

"Well. I wasn't sure what was going on either. But I think a man's house says a lot about him; especially a single man. And your house is really, really pretty. I don't mean pretty in a feminine way...I..."

"No. Pretty is good. Pretty is a compliment...Thank you...I was curious; before I step on any toes-is there anything happening between you and Moses?"

"No. Not at all. I only met him when I got here. He's a really nice guy. Our local affiliate assigned him to me for my work here. I think he's married. He always seems anxious to get back home anyway. But, Michael, before we get carried away here; you said there were a couple of things you had to tell me...", just then the waitress appears and interrupts,

"Hi, I'm Jennifer...", she is surprised with Michael's retort,

"Hi, I'm Michael...", which she ignores,

'I'll be your waitress. May I get you a drink?"

"Mary…why don't we go with the drink of the day; seabreezes OK with you? (She signifies-yes) Jennifer, two seabreezes."

"Great! I'll be right back with those."

Before they have a chance to peruse a menu; Skates appears to bus the table next to theirs.

"Dad, hey, what are you doing here?" Father and son hug in greeting.

"Son, I'd like you to meet Mary Diana…" Michael suddenly realizes that he has no idea of her last name,

"Is 'Diana' your last name? I don't even know." Mary turns to Skates,

"Hi Skates. I'm actually Maria Diana Magdalena. But Mary's just fine."

"Hi. How'd you know my name?"

"I even know where you sleep, young man. I'm a newswoman; I know all. (She says with a subtle smile thus endearing her immediately to Michael. It warms his heart to see a potential female friend befriend his son as he watches Skates' eyes widen at her 'knowledge'.) No …Really…I was one of the people who brought your Dad home the other night…after the attack."

"Ohh. So you're the pretty lady he talked about. 'Like an angel from heaven bathed in pure white light.' I think is what he said." Michael does a cringe grin while Skates and Mary crack up.

"OK son…Thanks for stripping away any façade I may have built up here. Don't you have some work to do?" Everybody's grinning as Skates returns to his task but he turns back with an unexpectedly serious glance toward his father,

"Dad, I've got my friends looking out for that as…that shmuck on the bike."

"Thanks. I'd like to talk to that kid." And Skates goes about his work. Mary asks,

"Is that all you'd like to do to that kid?"

"A karmic retaliation would probably involve setting him loose, alone, amongst a pack of wild hyenas since that is the unfeeling, selfish, ravenous carnivore his ilk remind me of most. And…since that isn't likely to happen…I'd like to teach him something…The cops don't care about twenty bucks and jail would just make him a more deadly, more professional thief. He's probably someone that could benefit from some insight into life if I can just get him to listen…Did I want to beat the crap out of him? Yes. I did. Part of me still would. But in just about every aspect of life you can choose between the physical and the Spiritual. Some people won't let you choose. They don't give you enough time to choose. If I'd have had a weapon the other night that kid could be dead right now. And for what…twenty bucks? It couldn't be worth it to him and I'd be a killer…in my own mind…forever. No. This lifetime I'm trying to make it through as clean as possible. A lot of people in my generation thought they could change the world. I still do. But now I just take it one person at a time."

"One person, one Love, one heart. Let's get together and feel all right…", Mary singingly mimics Bob Marley.

"Mary, how in the heck did you find your way to Mother Mary's Salvation Rib Station; you'd only been in town a really short time?"

"Moses. He's been down here a lot. And, after a long flight, some meaty protein peps me up. I try to keep my meat intake down. I'm not even sure I believe in eating meat. Killing animals and all. But, damn. Those ribs were *good.*"

"Yeah…Whitey and Mary definitely know how to cook. The music's great, too. I just love to hear Whitey play. Is that what inspired your musical outburst a minute ago?"

"Just a little play on words. Words are my stock in trade. I write all my own material, do my own research *and* deliver the goods on camera."

"Speaking of delivering the goods; here are our drinks." And the waitress re-appears,

"Have y'all decided what you want?"

"We really haven't looked yet. Mary, do you like pasta?"

"Sure do. I'm half Italian."

"I can recommend the tequila shrimp with lime-cilantro pasta. It's great. And believe me-a small order is plenty."

"It sounds great. I'll have that…and a field greens salad on the side."

"I try not to eat high carbo stuff anytime after lunch…so…I think I'll go with the snapper, blackened…and a small caesar salad." As the waitress departs, Michael resumes,

"I can't believe I've never seen you on TV. It's obvious you're gorgeous in person. (Mary smiles the smile of a woman fortunate enough for this sort of compliment to be the norm rather than the unusual.) And I'm sure on camera as well. But you know what kept running through my mind…and it took a while to even register…was your voice. (*This* gets her attention.) Many women have voices that irritate me; it doesn't even matter what the words are. The sound just grates on my ears. But your voice…It's like if you took a sound modulation machine and ran a scope of your voice; you could throw out the highs and the lows. (Michael pinches two fingers together and draws them through the air in front of him as if tracing an imaginary line.) There would be just this one center line. A direct line…through the middle. Straight to the heart of the matter."

"That's a really beautiful compliment. Thank you. Let's toast. To new voices in our lives. And…speaking of which-what the heck were you going to tell me?"

"Oh yeah. I did get just a teeny bit sidetracked, didn't I? Well, the people that own the Cadillac place also built the cross…and they're very protective of it. They now know that Rev. Baker is coming in tomorrow. And they've already asked to meet him. They don't know you're coming in. Do you think that Rev. Baker will know you by sight…Or maybe Mr. and Mrs. H., the owners, will?"

"I've never done a piece on Baker but I don't know the viewing habits of any of them. Do you think a confrontation at your work might be bad for you?"

"Well…possibly…" he says sheepishly.

"How about this? I won't bring Moses; but I will bring a little purse cam and mike…and maybe a little disguise. Subtle but effective. What do you think?"

"I appreciate it. I know it sounds chickenshit. But, it is my work du jour. And…at the moment-I need it. God, I hate the way that sounds."

"Don't worry. I understand. You've got your boy to think of…if nothing else…and I wouldn't want you to lose your job. At least not 'til I get my car…"

"You…are a funny girl. I like you. Have you been over to the cross yet?"

"Only peripherally. No camera. Just getting a feel for the people there."

"And what is that?"

"Lots of excitement, expectation. I hope they're not disappointed if things don't happen the way they want."

As their dinners are set before them; the warm fragrance of fresh cilantro wafts up toward Mary Diana's olfactory membranes,

"Ummm…good."

Michael wonders if the mere nuance of tequila in the dish will have any effect…

They talk over dinner into the night and get along famously. Afterwards, Michael walks Mary Diana the short distance to her hotel and continues walking home so that he may rest for tomorrow. He walks home alone purposefully and on purpose. He won't be deterred by that terd that accosted him the other night. As he's walking, he realizes he's feeling like a reporter on the trail of a hot story; instead of a salesman. It feels good. Who knows; he might even get the girl, too!

***

The next morning Michael is arranging papers on his desk; trying to get all in order for his deal today. Suddenly he notices the light from outside grow rapidly dim. He looks to the front as he hears a commotion beginning as people mumble excitedly. Looking out the window he spies the cause of the 'eclipse'. It must be Baker's bus. A huge commercial style bus with a custom paint job is blocking the sun from several windows of the showroom. As he rises up to go to the front, the bus features become clearer. He sees a gleaming gun-metal behemoth of a conveyance with a large haloed cross emblazoned on its grill. On its side is large yellow lettering that runs the length of the vehicle; reading

The Rev. TG Baker
Is Coming To Save You!

The lettering curves so that at the front end, under the high arch of **The Rev.**, etc., is a picture of Baker's face complete with high blonde maned hair so familiar to his viewers. At the other end, where the lettering curves down into '**To Save You**', is a picture, above the words, of Jesus with a haloed sword. The destination sign at the front top of the bus, that normally might read 'Cleveland' or some other town, reads,

ONE WAY

Through the darkened one-way glass of the side windows it's impossible to tell what's going on inside. Then the front door opens and a tall, imposing dark man emerges. Not a Black man; perhaps from the southern side of the Mediterranean. Middle Eastern? One thing's for certain; he looks more from a 'B' horror flick than a 'Christian' bus...and he's definitely not the reverend. The man has a black long greatcoat; like an Australian riding coat. He has a, almost handlebar type, moustache drooping down over a strong chin. His eyes are recessed; accenting a Rasputin-like aura.' He turns to assist the next person from the bus as he tosses away some sort of fast food wrapper on the ground. This must be Mrs. Baker emerging. Her wig of the day is a bright white shoulder length number. Her dress is a black A-line with a white pilgrim collar. Following her is the reverend himself. Mr. High and Mighty TG Baker. Only he's not so tall and he's enveloped in no cloud of glory. As he alights it becomes apparent that he's actually quite short and a bit portly. His face resembles Rush Limbaugh. Michael imagines that the hair is a theatrical device designed to make him appear taller. Filled with an instant revulsion Michael, never the less, rushes out to greet the reverend. He has to push off the other salespeople who, as is their custom, gravitate toward anything smelling of power or money.

"Get out of the way-he's here to save *me!*" And he forces his way out of the door.

"Rev. Baker, hello. I'm Michael Wade. Right this way, sir…"

Michael, Mr. and Mrs. Baker and the 'dark man' go to Michael's cubicle. Rev. Baker introduces his immediate entourage,

"Mr. Wade, this is my wife Elisha and this is my personal assistant Mr. Merdeces Tabarnac. Have you got everything ready for me? We don't know how long we've been called here for, so this must be an open-ended deal…all right, son?"

"Yes, sir. There is, of course, some paperwork that needs to be done. If you can fill out the particulars on yourself in these spaces that I've marked…everything else is ready to go. Oh, also…if you don't mind, the owner, Mr. Harrison, has asked to meet you. His family is quite influential around here and his wife's family built the cross you've come to see."

"Well, that would be wonderful, son. Just wonderful."

Michael's attention is diverted as he notices a woman with sunglasses, a scarf covering her head and wearing an overcoat (quite out of season) enter the building and converse with the greeter. He also notices George Suffian strangely eyeing the holy couple as if he may recognize them. Now there seems to be an argument developing up front with the lady who's just entered. 'Ohmigod', Michael thinks, 'that's Mary Diana.' He quickly excuses himself and hurries to the greeter's podium.

"Michael, this woman insists upon seeing you. I told her you were busy…"

"I'm sorry, Vivian. It's an unfortunate scheduling problem. It's my fault…"

Mary interjects,

"I'm Diana. I spoke to you on the phone about a used convertible."

"Yes, Certainly. If you don't mind, come back and sit in the office adjacent to mine while I finish with this customer."

As she nears the cubicle; she feigns excitement upon seeing the Bakers,

"Praise God! Rev. and Mrs. Baker. I watch you all the time. You're so speshul (she affects a southern accent) to me and millions of others."

"Well child, thank you. Have you joined the COG; our Circle Of Givers?"

"Not yet reverend; but just as soon as I get a few more pennies together I most certainly will. Especially after being *personally* invited by you…And Mrs. Baker…you are such an inspiration to the women of America. Setting the example for Christian women."

As she speaks, the reverend has gotten up and is giving his new 'fan' a distinctly non-Christian hug. Then Mrs. Baker joins her husband in the love-fest/grope. Merdeces eyes the intruder suspiciously. Rev. Baker offers,

"Here dear. Sit here while we tidy up some business." Maria sits and continues,

"Reverend, what are you doing in this little community?"

"My dear, as usual, we are here to root out evil and to raise the name of the Lord in praise! Are you from here?"

"No, sir. Just visiting some friends."

"We plan on holding some revivals here. Will you join us?"

"Why I'd be honored, sir."

Michael's getting nervous in the middle of this charade and says,

"Rev. Baker, why don't we go meet Mr. Harrison?"

"All right, Merdeces, stay here will you?" he orders.

Michael and the Bakers go back to the office of Mr. H.

"Sir, this is Rev. and Mrs. Baker...my boss, Mr. Harrison." Harrison's imposing presence and complimentary voice bids them welcome,

"Well, it's nice to have some celebrities in town. (Indeed, many famous people have visited here and a few even live here; but this is as close as a small town Cadillac dealer usually gets.) Y'all are very highly thought of around here. Have a seat." He motions to the commodious leather chairs fronting his desk.

Michael returns to his desk just in time to hear Merdeces ask Mary,

"You look familiar. How might I know you?" as he leans menacingly close to Mary,

"I don't know. Have you ever been to Jacksonville?"

"No", he responds dryly,

"Where are you from?"

"Deir Sunbol."

"The sunbelt..." Mary queries trying to understand. Michael, over-hearing, thinks it sounded like some sort of salutation; but he doesn't care. He wants to extract Mary from her identity crisis before she's prematurely discovered.

"Diana, come...let me show you the car I was telling you about." Grateful for the intervention she quickly follows him to the used car area leaving Tabarnac intently eyeing them as they exit.

"Sorry Mary. I was getting nervous there. Do you think that weird guy knew who you were?"

"Hard to tell; but I'd hate to meet him in an alley on a dark night. Daylight's bad enough."

"Meeting him gives me a bad feeling...you ever had that...a feeling when you meet someone that will negatively effect your life? You don't know how...you don't know when...just a creepy, evil feeling."

"Forewarned is forearmed..."

"I'll start working out...but seriously folks-what do you want to do? Try and get some more info or look at the car?"

"I wish there were some way to hear what's going on in your boss's office..."

"Maybe there is. They hardly ever give the phone girl a break. Let me see if she needs to pee and I'll offer to catch the phones. Maybe I can hear something through the intercom. You trail me. If she doesn't want to get up; then you come up and ask her to show you the way to the bathroom. Act dumb; like you can't find it, OK?"

"OK."

They head toward the phone desk wo-manned by a girl in her late teens,

"Barb, you want a break? I'm kinda waiting for my customer to get through talking to Mr. H."

"You must've heard my bladder calling. Thanks Michael. I'll be right back."

"Take your time." Michael is nervous about this; what if he gets caught? It's really an invasion of privacy. What the hey. He's a pretend reporter right now. He punches some buttons and hopes he's got it; without broadcasting whatever he's punched up to the entire dealership. Yes; he can hear them. Now; should he take notes? He's new at this. He hears Mr. H. speaking,

"Have you talked to the church officials about your intentions?"

"No, Mr. Harrison. We just got here...and of course, no offense, but that is a Catholic Church. We'll probably have a few prayer meetings at the cross and set up our big revival tent at the park down the street."

"Perhaps I could assist you with the city fathers in obtaining any required permits."

"That would be very fine of you. Very fine of you."

Just then Barb returns from her brief break and Michael clumsily fumbles with the phones as he hurries to cover up his eavesdropping.

"Thanks Michael. I thank you and my plumbing thanks you."

He backs out of the space hoping he's left no trace of his mission. He sidles up to Mary and whispers as they head back to the cubicle that he hadn't heard much in that short time. They notice that the 'dark man' has gone elsewhere and Michael takes this opportunity to show Mary the paperwork that Baker has filled out.

"Wow. Mary, look at the gross income he's got listed here. Damn. I knew they must be racking up the bucks. But this is just one year."

"Yes. And that's just what's on the books, probably. These 'revivals' rake in a lot of cash. I can't imagine this flake reporting it all." As they're huddled over the paperwork; Tabarnac suddenly returns,

"I'll take that for my boss. Please." 'Please' from this man sounds different than from the lips of most people.

Shortly thereafter, Harrison and the Bakers emerge. Mr. H. charges Michael, "Please give every courtesy to Rev. Baker during his stay. Now, please…show them to their cars."

Out front the impressively long limos are lined up. The Rev. and Mrs. Baker get into the lead black car with Tabarnac at the wheel. The second car takes two women, one White and one Black. Three accountant types in black suits get into the third car. As they begin to pull away; Tabarnac turns to the back of his limo to tell something to Baker. Michael sees the window of Baker's limo roll down so that he can just see his eyes…glaring at him over the rim of the glass as they head down the street towards the cross.

As Michael and Mary go back to his cubicle they talk as they walk,

"I think that Tabarnac guy suspects something's up with us", Michael alleges.

"Well, he's right. Isn't he?" she answers with a sly grin eliciting a double take from her possible doublespeak,

"Whatever way you meant that; I'd have to say yes. Say, want to go by the cross at sundown? I can't guarantee what we'll see; but I could, at least, introduce you to Father Leonard. He seems like a nice guy."

"Sure. Now. About my car…"

They, again, walk out to the used car lot. And there it is. An immaculate 1987 red Cadillac El Dorado with red leather interior and a white top. Mary instantly loves it. Mary takes it.

"Mary's going to pick you up in this tonight, OK?"

"I'll see you back here at 6."

Arroz con Pollo Simpatico (Friggin' Chickasee)

❀

In 2-quart shallow baking dish, mix one can condensed cream of mushroom soup, one cup water. ¾ cup uncooked rice of your choice, teaspoon of hot Hungarian paprika and ground pepper to taste. Place 4 skinless, boneless chicken breast halves on top and color with sprinkle of additional paprika and pepper. Cover. Bake at 375 degrees for 45 minutes. Add freshly sliced circles of green, red and yellow bell peppers when done. Serve.

Zesty Duckling

(This was contributed by my good friend,
June Canard of Montreal)

This is a good Holyday dish. But why wait!

Heat your oven to 350 degrees.

Cut a lemon into fourths and rub the outside of a large duckling with one quarter. Chuck it.

Separately, in a small mixing bowl, mix together the zest of the rest of the lemon with the zest of one orange and 1 tbsp. freshly grated ginger. Rub this on the inside of the duck. Now fill the cavity with the remaining citrus pieces, reserving the juice. Place duck on rack in roaster and sprinkle with sea salt and white pepper.

If you haven't enough juice left, add to the small mixing bowl juice to equal ¼ cup lemon juice and ½ cup orange juice. To this, add 4 tbsp. grapeseed oil, 2 tbsp. grated ginger and 3 tbsp. orange blossom honey or maple syrup. Use this to baste several times during the hour or so it will take for the duck juices to run clear when the thigh is pierced with a fork. Remove from oven and baste one final time while the duck cools sufficiently to carve. (about 10 minutes.)

CHAPTER FOUR

Medea

Cruising down the road on a sunny day in Florida in a Cadillac convertible. What could be finer?!

Screeeech!!!

Mary brakes hard at the police barricade a block from the church; almost throwing Michael through the windshield.

"Jesus…What's going on?" Michael says, feeling his head to see if his wound opened.

"I'm sorry. You OK? I was…lost in thought there…"

A police officer approaches,

"Sorry, ma'am. We've had to block off this road for a few hours. There's a crowd gathering at the church. We don't know how big it's going to get…you folks going there, too?"

"Yes sir. How many people are there?"

"I'd say about a hundred right now…but with that story in the paper we think it may get wild later. You can go down Seminole Avenue and park along there if you like."

"Thanks officer."

As they pull onto Seminole and park, Michael says,

"Looks like you got to town just in time."

"Maybe so…maybe so. You know, if Baker's there; very quickly he'll know that you and I aren't just salesman and customer…Are you all right with that?"

"Look, Mary…I know we just met…and Lord knows where that will go; but I hate my job. Hate's a strong word. I dislike my job intensely. I find little there to be proud of…to care about…or anything. So, if Mr. H or Rev. B has a problem with my liking an intelligent, articulate, beautiful woman…Well; that would just confirm what I think of them…Better broke than broken. I'll work at Burger King. Let's go."

"Mr. H might own the Burger King, too…"

"There's that humor again…Come on. Hey; what about your cameraman?"

"I'll call Mose on my cellular while we're walking over. It's hard to keep him on call all the time. You ever handle a camera?"

"Not a handheld; but I've run one several times when I took an acting class in Miami."

"Let me call Moses and suggest something to him…" and she dials Moses.

A party mood seems to be prevailing as they approach the church. It's hard to tell what's going on up front, nearer to the cross. But the rear of the group shows evidence of alcohol consumption accompanied by the inevitable blare of a boom box or two turned to a, not too, ear shattering level. Out of respect? Michael spots Father Leonard and Sister Grace perusing the crowd. Lenny has a slightly concerned look on his face as they approach,

"Father, Sister. Hi, Michael Wade. I met you here recently."

One after the other they respond

"Hi Michael." "Welcome back."

"This is my friend, Mary Diana." Michael asks Leonard,

"What do you think, Father? This is just going to get bigger and bigger, isn't it?"

"It certainly seems that way. At least until a message is delivered or a hoax is declared…or God knows what."

"Father. Have you heard that TG Baker plans on holding rallies here?"

"He's right over there. (Leonard gives a quick head glance indicating Bakers presence across the crowd.) I can't say he impresses me. At least not positively."

"How do you feel about his being here, though?" Mary wants to know.

"This area here is church property. Without our permission he can't hold meetings right here. But that patch from the street to the cross is public access. And that patch over there, where the old graveyard is, is city property...a park...a tourist attraction. We can't really control those areas. The church property picks up again, over there, on the far side near the gift shop and the church offices. To answer your question more directly; I wish he weren't here. Grace, what do you think?"

"I wish only the truly devout would come. Those who simply wish to pray...and enjoy the solitude of this place. I've seen that Rev. Baker on television and I think of him more as a circus performer than a man of God."

Michael's pretty sure he knows the answer to his next question; but it isn't often he's had an opportunity to get it straight from the vicar's mouth,

"I'm not Catholic...and this may sound impertinent; but I really am curious. Why are you a Father and you only a Sister...not a Mother...?"

Grace fields this as if she's not unused to the question,

"We have our Mother Superiors, etc...but the head of the Church is a man..."

Leonard adds,

"It's all biblical. Let's face it. The Church recognizes Mary as the Mother of our Lord...and venerates her for it; but it hasn't yet extended that to recognition of women as direct equals with men."

The attention of the four is drawn away as the crowd noise increases and their focus becomes the cross...as, near land but over the edge of the bay, a cloud forms to the left as the sun begins it's westward run. Just as the sun hits the cross beam it seems that an image of a face appears in the cloud that now moves directly behind the top of the cross. The crowd gasps. Boomboxes and beer cans drop to the ground. Many people drop to their knees. Some sob.

"Fall down and **repent??**" a booming voice thunders above the silent din…It's TG Baker holding a wireless mike and standing on a rise off to the left near some olive trees,

"Hear the word of the Lord. You have seen His glorious face. You **must** believe! You, who would know the Lord, be at the park tomorrow before sundown and hear what God has in store for you!! From there we will march to the cross at sunset to see our Lord once again. **Glory Hallelujah!!**"

Baker wades into the crowd. Laying on hands as people jerk and fall to the ground. It looks as if the sea of bodies before him has parted to make way for His Hairship.

Mary spots Moses with his local Channel 11 crew and calls out to him, "Mose, what did you get?"

"Some beautiful pictures of a sunset and the rantings of some false prophet…I think"

"I left a message for you. Got a minute?"

"Sure."

"Listen, I know you're stretched three ways from Sunday trying to help me and do your regular stuff and living thirty miles away. I've got an idea that might help both of us. Do you think you can get me a camera to use while I'm here?"

"Yes, I think I could. Do you have someone to operate it?"

"Remember that guy that got bonked on the head?" she says pointing back toward Michael…Moses shakes his head and says,

"Look. I'll get you a camera. But there's no way it'll look like broadcast quality without a pro."

"He's got some experience. Maybe you could just give him a couple of pointers."

"Well. It would help me out. But it's your ass and I know nothing. Nothing. OK?"

"You got it. Do you think you can bring it down tomorrow?"

"Shouldn't be any problem. They're definitely going to be covering this for a few days…could go wide."

"Call me at the hotel tomorrow and we'll hook up. Thanks Moses. Thanks a lot." Moses turns back to his local anchor, Alele Porfiria. She's a young, extremely light skinned Black woman. If it weren't for some subtle Negroid features; she could easily pass. She has her hair pulled back and has on a typical newswoman's suit. They do their wrap-up and prepare to leave as Mary walks back toward Michael.

"Hey, Beanie Baby. How'd you like to be in the reporting game?"

"Beanie Baby?"

"Moses will get us a camera. Think you can handle it?"

"If you've got anything to do with it; I'll definitely give it a shot… Beanie Baby?"

"Speaking of beans; my Cuban roots are calling. Anyplace around here we can get some black beans and rice?"

"Actually…yes. I think so. So you're an Italian-Cuban combo, huh? Interesting. Very in-ter-est-ing. Black beans and rice. I can't think of a Cuban place; but there is a great little Mexican place over on the water."

Yes. What could be better than cruising along on a sunny Florida day? How about cruising along the Florida coast after the sun's set and it cools off a bit. Salt air, top down.

"Mary. Do you know you can actually drive on the beach here? Pull down that road over there and let's cruise the beach."

Screeeech!!!

Michael's almost slammed again.

"Sorry Mary. I guess I should have given you a tad more warning. Do you think God's trying to pound something into my head? Are you his messenger? First, the kid on the bike. And now, two bangs in one day."

"Wow. This is cool", Mary says as they pull onto the sand; pretty much ignoring his allusion to her driving.

It is pretty, too. There's a low moon hanging over the sea; the waves gently rush onto shore. Quiet. No traffic. Michael leans back and enjoys the moment. Another resting place in eternity.

"There is pleasure; there is joy. Know the difference", he says to himself as much as anyone.

"Mary, I'm going to give you some warning here and I'm going to brace myself. See that lighted area up ahead? That's where we're headed. So, slow down…gradually…please…" he says almost begging.

"I guess I never learned to do that too well. Always fast forward; full speed ahead…maybe I should try learning to slow down some… gradually…"

She successfully slows to a stop at the restaurant without smashing Michael. The sign on the quaint seaside bistro reads,

Lucia y Francisco's
Foods of Mexico
&
Tapas Bar

The couple see no need to go any further than the deck overlooking the beach. Simple wooden tables and benches. Colored lights strung along the eaves of the main structure. Not too many; just enough to give a festive air to the place. Many people don't think of Mexicans when they think of Florida. In truth, there are many here. Quite a few live in the small agricultural towns that ring Lake Okeechobee. Most of those people came, originally, to harvest crops. Many also come north for business and for the tourist destinations. Authentic Mexican food is readily available here. A waitress approaches dressed in semi-native costume. A white cotton dress accented with multi-hued ribbons woven through the fabric horizontally,

"Hello. Some food tonight?"

"Yes. Do you think you can satisfy the Cuban half of this woman's appetite with some black beans and rice?"

"I think so. Con pollo?" "No thanks." And you, sir?"

"I'll have the cheese enchiladas and…Sangria OK with you, Mary?"
Mary nods in assent and the waitress leaves to place the order.

"Maria Diana Magdalena. So, are you Mary Magdalene?"

"I've never had seven demons cast out of me; but both halves of my family were nominal Catholics. So, I'm sure the thought must have been there. You know there is remarkably little said about her in the Bible. You hear all kinds of stuff about how she was a prostitute and all. I can't find it in the Bible. Maybe I should try to be more like the Mother Mary Mary instead of the Mary Magdelene Mary."

"How do you mean?"

"Oh, I'm not sure. The past couple of years I've felt strongly that a soul wants to come through me. A child."

"Really. How did this come to pass?"

"I couldn't explain it. I don't even know if it's true. It may just be that I'm a woman and *think* I'm supposed to give birth. I don't know… nothing concrete…just a very strong feeling." The food arrives,

"Here Mother Mary; eat up. You're going to need your strength. First we must battle the evil false prophet…and then…we'll have to work on that other issue."

Their eyes lock. And they smile at the possibilities. Michael switches gears,

"Speaking of false prophets; did you catch what TG stands for? Tipper Gaye Baker. Strange name."

"Yes. And his wife's name is Elisha. You'd think with the income they put down on your credit form that she could afford some wigs that, at least, *looked* like real hair. They look like floss…"

"Dental?"

"No, like cotton candy. Wigs are stupid anyway. I mean maybe some highlights or color…but cheap, dyed wigs? Maybe she thinks it creates some sort of bond with some of her back-woodsy flock. Ugly."

"Truly. So…what's your next move; storywise?"

"I'll go to the 'rally' tomorrow and follow the Baker's charade parade to the cross…openly. I've got to let them know I'm with the media. If you're in on this with me, like you've said, they'll know you're with me."

"Actually, I'm looking forward to it. Some guys can do the sales thing. But tell me, how can anyone sell something to another person with true passion unless it's selfish passion. The passion to make as much off each customer as possible…the passion to feed himself and his family…I mean…they make fun of their customers. That's not the kind of passion I want…I want passion for life; from life. I want passion of the Spirit; the soul. I want passion motivated by Love. A search for truth, knowledge."

"It sounds like you've got it. That's one thing about my job that I love. I get to go after things. I get to pursue truth. I hate to do fluff. Of course, I had to cover a lot of fluff to get where I am now. But…I got to travel…a lot. I got to meet people…of all varieties. I don't know where it's all going…but, it's a pretty great run up the mountain…want to come along."

"Let's see how it goes. But…it sounds great."

They finish dinner with a new awareness of why they are attracted to each other. They both have passion. They both seek the truth. Not a bad premise for a relationship.

As Michael gets back inside his house he flips on the news on the living room TV and sticks his head into Skates' room to say hello. Skates is asleep in the midst of schoolbooks scattered on his bed and MTV blaring from his TV. Michael flicks off Skates TV and goes back to the living room to see what Moses' Channel ll team caught today. They lead off with the 'Miracle in San Jacinto' story. Alele Porfiria, the Black albino female reporter that was with Moses earlier today, is speaking,

"Today, at the tallest cross on the eastern seaboard near the spot where Spanish explorers first landed in the new world, a strange phenomenon occurred. At sundown, on the grounds of the Church of Nuestra Senora de la Leche Perpetuo, some say a vision of Christ appeared in a cloud behind the top of the cross. The cross was erected by the Agrippa family of San Jacinto some thirty years ago. Channel 11 News was there today. Judge for yourself as we show you this footage. As you can see, the sun made a brilliant flash of light on the old cross… and it *is* dramatic. Is it a miracle? Rev. TG Baker, of televangelism fame, thinks so. He announced he would hold a 'faith rally' tomorrow at City Park and then lead a march to the cross to ask Christ to come again and be received. We'll be here tomorrow to bring you that story. Alele Porfria for Channel 11 News." They close their coverage with a shot of Baker waving from the back of his limo. Michael's first thought is that this will bring a lot of reporters to town. He dials Mary's room,

"316, please. Mary? Hope I didn't wake you."

"No, Just lying here in bed watching the news. Did you watch?"

"Yes. That was my motive for calling. I think the town may begin to fill up with your peers soon. Very soon. I wouldn't be surprised if they started getting here tomorrow."

"That could be. But…more than likely they'll use local reporters for a national feed…or just run tape. It's not that big a story yet. No one even has a picture of anything that looks like Christ. Now, if he does appear; that *will* be a story. Of course, it may be the last story ever told if this is judgement day and we all go up in the rapture."

"And now, reporting from purgatory-Mary Magdalene!" Michael mocks,

"What if it's all true? What *is* true? Heaven, hell, damnation, Jesus…why isn't it made more plain for us?"

"I don't know…maybe God will come to apologize for confusing us. 'He ain't dead; he's just on the nod' ", he says quoting a line from an old Danny O'Keefe song.

"Michael, I'll call you at work tomorrow as soon as I hear when Moses can get us a camera. Let's mediate on all this as we sleep."

"Did you know that tapas, like the tapas bar we were at tonight, has another meaning?"

"No, what's that?"

"In the ancient Hindu texts called the Upanishads; tapas means the power of meditation. So. As we have partaken of tapas; let us use this for meditative power as we sleep."

"You…are a funny man. I think I like you."

"I like you, too. Sleep tight. Hasta manana."

"Good night Michael", she says softly as she gathers the covers around her.

Sub 4-1
TG's Jesus

Baker is sleeping contentedly in his suite a few floors above when he hears a voice in the darkness,

"Prepare the way. Soon I will come. Soon I will deliver my message at the cross. A new message for a new age." The voice is gentle, but deep and commanding. Baker dares to open his eyes as he peeks over the edge of his covers. There, hovering, is an apparition. It's Baker's Jesus. A faint transparent image looms just beyond the foot of the bed. Baker is temporarily paralyzed. He cannot move; but he pays rapt attention. How could he not? Baker's Jesus has a crown of thorns that pierce the forehead causing small trickles of blood to seep down the face that mix with the slightest hint of tear water emerging from the corner of an eye. The blood and water merge upon Jesus' face. His look is anguished and far away as if his words come from another source beyond even him,

"You will call the people to be there; but you shall ask for no payment. Your reward is coming. Hear me. You shall ask for no payment. Your reward is coming. Do you hear? Do you agree?" Achingly, hesitantly, but triumphantly, he answers,

"Yes, Lord. I hear. I agree", then Baker dares to inquire, "You won't be there tomorrow?"

The vision fades as Elisha stirs next to him,

"Tip, what's going on? Can't you sleep?" Baker attempts to respond but is having difficulty finding the words,

"Lisha…Jesus just delivered a message…to me…personally…"

"What? Was He 90 feet tall or…"

"No, no. He was here. He spoke to *me*." He flips on the bedside light. Elisha is bald and has a hint of a five o'clock shadow.

"He spoke to *me*…but…He won't be there tomorrow."

"We've come all this way for…"

"No. He'll be here soon; but not tomorrow. He said we must prepare the way. We must call the faithful…" his tone changes as he adds,

"But…we can't collect any money…"

"What!? Is He nuts?"

"We must obey. Our reward is guaranteed by Jesus himself."

TG turns to his faithful companion (Trigger?) and he/she says,

"I will not leave you", and they embrace as he turns out the light.

***

The following day Mary Diana has secured a video camera from Moses. She's now showing Michael its operation as they meet prior to the revival/march. The camera has some unfamiliar features but he gets the hang of it very quickly.

"There. You think you've got it?"

"Yeah, We'll be OK. Let's go cover this circus." The full circus atmosphere that will develop hasn't yet. But there is a tent that Baker's people have erected in the city park. The tent is huge and shelters the large gathering from the brutal sun. As the news team of Michael and Mary make their way toward the big-top, they see Moses' crew across the way as well as many other media folk sprinkled throughout the crowd. There are reporters, sound trucks and cameras representing various media, both print and TV. However, the largest contingent is of Baker's own staff. It appears they, alone, have enough equipment to film a decently budgeted Hollywood blockbuster. Michael makes his first shot of Baker's crowd workers as they distribute 'Bible Gum.' These are small squares of ordinary bubble gum except on the outside covering it is an image of Baker in full rant. The inside cover bears a Bible verse. Does it come in sugar-free, he wonders, for the spiritually obese? Or is it, perhaps, to give a sugar rush to the Holy Spirit. Holy Spirit Gum, Batman!

Baker begins,
"Friends! We are gathered here today to march as the body of Christ. We march to the CROSS-! We march to see the *signs* in the *heavens!* March to see the face of Christ!" Hallelujahs and Glory Be's fill the air as the crowd feels it is blessed to be in this place at this moment.
"Brothers and Sisters…will you join me?!"
'*Yes, Brother!*'
"Will you join me as we march?!"
'*Yassir, Lead us!*'
"Will you join me as we march to see Jesus in the sky?!"
'*Praise God, we will!*'
"My name is TG Baker! THANK GOD!"
'*Thank God, Rev. Baker, thank God!*'
"My life has been devoted to healing the sick and spreading the word. Do you need help? (*Yes!*) Are you saved (*Yes!*) If you're saved, you have your help. If you're saved, you have what you need. If you want to be saved; *raise* your hand and raise it *high!*" Near the stage, a cluster of hands immediately pierce the air. "Remember, you can always be saved again just as you can be born again. The Day of Atonement is nigh. Everyone desiring to be saved-*form a line-to the right of the stage!*" About thirty potential converts line up as Baker once again lays on hands and lays waste as bodies drop at his feet. Aids attend the fallen. Do they fall from the power of his touch? From the power of his perception? From deception? Or from their own expectation? He mounts the stage once more to exhort the crowd,

"Now, every-one-up on stage! Every one in the audience…march across the stage. Follow me! As we march to Jesus.

Gather together in my name,

Saith the Lord

And march with me

March with me to see

The Glo-ry; the Glo-ry of God!

Follow me!!" The crowd follows him up one side and down the other; out into the street and toward the cross. Mary glances at Michael,

"He didn't even mention money…donations, nada."

"Yeah, weird, huh?"

"Not his style. Maybe he'll make a pitch at the cross."

"Mary, aren't you going to ask how I did?" He says as eagerly as a kid at Christmas.

"The proof is in the video. We'll play it back in the room, OK…", she says not really asking as she breaks into a trot. Michael hurries to stay even with her as they hustle to be at the front of the crowd. They want the best position for the best shots. Michael senses that they must be starting to look like a team; running in tandem with a common goal as he thinks, 'This is cool'. Mary thinks, 'Damn these high heels'. Now they're at the front of the pack, catching up with a few other crews. They're pacing backwards, preceding the action, when they realize they're in sync with Moses. Michael shouts over, gesturing with his shouldered camera,

"Thanks for the equipment!"

"You're welcome."

"Have a drink with us later."

"Catch me after the 'show'."

The minor media frenzy continues backpedaling like a ragtag football team in pass defense drill. Baker's leading the parade as he wedges back the news crews; forcing them away from the center as the crowd nears its goal. He stares directly into each camera, daring them to belittle his mission. His currently patient and docile wife strides beside him as they lead the crowd to the very foot of the cross. The sun is drawing closer to the far side of the earth and anticipation grows. As the hour draws nigh, a distinct hush falls upon the crowd. The weighty silence becomes so heavy as to seem audible.

Michael begins to inwardly, silently chant. Mostly from nervousness and the oppressive silence. His chant is drawn from two sources. The first is a loud inner 'hmmm' that starts at the top of the rear of his tongue and resonates up through the top of his head. This is an exercise often employed by public speakers, actors, telemarketers, etc...it gives their voices an internal warm-up so that when they finally open their mouths to emit sound they are already 'on'; at pitch. He decides this will do no good for this moment and he switches to 'Huuuu'. An open-ended, unending 'Huuuu' that can go on as long as the breath can hold. This sound he learned a few years ago as a spiritual exercise taught by members of Eckankar (Literally, the way of the eternal.) Their belief is that all sound, all vibration is the sound of the universe. Even scientists agree that, always, there is an underlying background sound to the universe. Attuning to this sound is how one plugs in to the universe. Michael isn't certain of the ultimate validity of all this. He knows it makes him calmer. And it does make him feel connected to the source of Life. This sound begins deep in the body. From the heart of sound; the diaphragm. It then works it's way up and out. When just the right pitch is reached; he feels aligned with the universe. Hu, he feels, is even capable of correcting problems in the body. He's nervous. He needs this.

The sun reaches the point where it should send out its dying rays for one last grasp at life as it clings to the cross beam. It does not disappoint.

Bam,

Bang,

Blinded by the light.

The crowd is awed...but there is no cloud...there is no image.

Baker has moved near the grove of olive trees with his cordless mike,

"Hearing you will hear and not understand.

Seeing you will see and not perceive.

Lest they should understand with their hearts and turn,

So that I should heal them.

Praise the Lord!" The crowd receives this hesitantly. They don't know what is transpiring. Did they fail to see? Is their faith not strong enough? (Have they been found out?)

"Hear me, oh ye of little faith. You *shall* be witnesses. Soon we will once again come to this spot. We *shall* see Jesus…But we must prepare. Now, return to the tent of the Lord and we will lift up our voices in prayer and song. Day and night, we will prepare…the way…of the Lord."

Afterwards, Moses, Mary and Michael meet for a brew at the Brew House. Moses asks,

"How'd it go Mr. Cameraman?"

"Nothing like your work, I'm sure."

"What'd you think of the 'show', Mary?"

"Kind of wait and see…"

"Does he have some sort of grand plan?", Michael puzzles.

"I think I should get an interview with Baker…", Mary almost silently states.

"What happened to wait and see?", Moses asks as Mary comes out of her reverie.

"I waited…and I has seen the light!", Mary blurts out, giggling, almost blowing her beer and causing the guys at the table to chortle. As normalcy resumes, Moses excuses himself to leave,

"Look guys. That's my one beer. I'm headed up. I'll let you know what our next move is."

"Moses. When you've got a few minutes, I'd appreciate some tips on camera work."

"No problem. I'll let you know."

Now, it's just the two of them. And Mary's curious about her beer buddy. "I've told you something of my history, raised in Newark, started in New York, went to LA, my folks still live in Jersey and so on…What about you? Excluding Skates, do you have any family?"

"No. Not for years. My folks died when I was twenty-one…"

"At the same time?" Strangely, Michael bares a slight grin at this normally grim enquiry. "Why are you smiling?' she says, incredulous.

"I'm sorry. You see, my folks were great. They gave me Love. They taught me Love. Something I hope to bequeath to my son. That they're dead makes me sad. The way they died…I'm sorry…it makes me laugh. (Mary's mouth is dropping as her eyes widen.) Let me explain…before you think I'm totally weird. I couldn't laugh at this if I didn't believe my parents died with a grin on their faces. My Dad was an air force pilot…though he always encouraged my pacifist leanings…he had seen war; he didn't want me to have to see it. Mostly, I was raised in Corpus Christi, Texas before we moved to a little town near Cape Canaveral called Christmas, Florida. After my Dad got his twenty, we moved to south Florida…they got the house of their dreams. Beautiful place, on a canal, terraced landscaping, dock, the whole bit…including a Jacuzzi…by the pool…outside…overlooking the waterway. Our first full night there; I went out…to check out the town…and my folks decided to celebrate; I guess. You see, they really Loved each other. They were naked in the Jacuzzi when I got back. There was something wrong with the wiring. They were electrocuted. Maybe I'm putting this spin on it to avoid pain; I don't know. But I prefer to remember them as two people in Love; after that many years…I mean they had these grins on their faces…and I believe they're happy where ever they are. I call it coitus interruptus electricus…and I smile. Sad, sick…I don't know. It's like they stayed around just long enough to raise me to maturity and then-bang-they were gone. Like they had given me this foundation of Love…to live my life…coitus interruptus electricus-they were gone. But I smile when I miss them" Mary is confused and fascinated and finally accepting of his good intentions; but she can't imagine ever thinking anything of her parents like this.

"Michael...I can imagine this; but I can't conceive of this...Can I absorb this for a while?"

"Sure. I've never told anyone but you and Skates...and after seeing that look on your face; I know why." The impasse is passed as Mary changes the subject,

"Listen. Will you call Baker for me...tell him I want an interview?..."

Mussels Marinara

For the sauce, you'll need finely sliced, chopped vegetables.

1 large red onion.

6 stalks celery (with leaves).

6 carrots.

About 4lbs. fresh ripe tomatoes.

In a large saucepan, heat 1-cup good olive or grapeseed oil and add veggies. Add 1/3 cup chopped garlic. Cook and constantly stir. As they're cooking, spice with lots of freshly torn basil leaves, oregano and thyme. Also add 4 large fresh bay leaves (untorn). Add a half bottle red vermouth or Moite Moite and constantly stir over medium heat for 20-30 minutes. To taste, add a few crushed Italian red peppers.

When the sauce is reduced to a delectable consistency, transfer to large pot that's big enough to hold 2-3 lbs. of your freshly obtained washed, scrubbed and de-bearded mussels. Be sure they're fresh. Know your dealer!

Add mussels to pot with sauce and keep heating 'til mussels yield and open. Ahhh.

CHAPTER FIVE

Room at the Inn

The Casa Maria Hotel is the only lodging available in San Jacinto that can lay claim to *anything* like a 5-star rating. It's only been re-opened as a hotel for the past year after serving for decades as a government edifice. Like most downtown buildings; it is historic. Originally it was built as a hotel to rival the hotels of Henry Flagler. Flagler was the millionaire oilman that put San Jacinto and much of Florida on the map around the turn of the century by building hotels and a railroad. The railroad eventually reached its terminus in the southernmost city in the continental U.S., Key West. But San Jacinto was in the far north of the state and thus received earlier attention. What's odd is that Flagler didn't particularly care all that much for the historical aspects of the city. He wanted to bring rich, cold northerners down for the winter. He's even credited with destroying many older structures to build *his* structures. The irony is that, now his buildings are historic and **they** are attractions. His grandest hotel is just across the street from the Casa Maria and, while still standing, is no longer a hotel, but is an institution of higher learning. The Casa Maria first opened in the early part of the 20th century but simply wasn't able to compete effectively with Flagler's cross-street rival hotel. One error made by the original builder was encasing the plumbing in concrete. This made is difficult and expensive to repair any water related problems. Eventually the property went into bankruptcy and Flagler bought it for a song.

But after the turn of the century hoopla; Flagler's rich, cold northerners moved further south to warmer climes and San Jacinto became an almost forgotten dot on the north Florida map. After several decades, as Flagler's buildings aged and they, themselves, became historic, tourists began returning in the form of history buffs, school groups and the like. In fact it's difficult to find a person who attended primary school in Florida in the past 30 years that didn't make at least one school sponsored trip here. More recently the little town had begun to attract European tourists (who often knew more of it's history than most Americans) and people making a side trip from Disney World as well as the beach-seeking folks. If you drive just a short distance from the heart of the city; these days you will find typical boxy condos, occupied by rich cold northerners and Canadians, with guarded gated entries and the water view completely out off from public sight. If it weren't for the strict historical protection laws and the huge state run beachfront park; those disgustingly ugly condom-minimums would be marching straight up to and over the 400-year-old fort that overlooks Serapis Bay. Never say the government didn't do something good for San Jacinto.

This renewed interest in the city led a group of investors to buy the old Casa Maria and turn it into something resembling the charm of it's heyday. They had it totally gutted and refurbished while actually enhancing its original elegant Spanish architecture. The rooms even retain the often-odd patterns that allowed them to be fit to various curves of the building. The top two twin turret tower rooms are two story suites. Each has it's own curving carpeted wooden staircase with brass handrails. There is a hot tub on the upper level of each of these suites with a small porthole window from which to view the town. At seven stories, the Casa Maria is (by one story) the second tallest building within the city limits. It is these two suites that are now occupied by the Bakers and Tabarnac and to which Michael now places a call.

'Casa Maria, how may I direct your call?', a feminine voice answered in what had become the standard business telephone greeting of the modern era. They used the same greeting at Cadillac. Michael couldn't stand it. For one thing, it was too commonly used. For another, what the hell did they mean 'direct your call?'

"Hi, this is Michael Wade for TG Baker, please."

"Just a moment and I'll connect you."

A voice, sounding much like Bakers, answers in the room. Due to the rhythmic grunting of the voice and the loud sound of rushing water in the background, Michael has to ask,

"Is this Mr. Baker?" (He has decided to avoid using the title 'Reverend' wherever possible regarding Baker as he considers it almost blasphemous.)

"uh…huh…What…do you…want?"

"Sir, this is Michael Wade…from the Cadillac store. I've gotten involved with a woman from a national news program that would like to interview you and Mrs. Baker regarding your 'mission' here. Would this afternoon around 5:30 be convenient?"

"uh..huh…Where…?"

"How about the band shell in the downtown plaza?"

"The…cross…"

"Well, sir. The cross is so tall it wouldn't even fit in the shot. How about downtown instead?"

"5…..30"

"Sir, are you OK?"

"5….30"

"Yes, sir…5.30." As Michael hangs up he's trying to figure out the odd cadence with which Baker spoke. 'Oh, well', he thinks, '5:30'.

Shortly after Baker hangs up his hotel extension; there is a knock that is, at first, unheard. If one had looked up from the street at this time they would have seen Baker's head gazing out the porthole window and thrusting back and forth in the same rhythmic pattern as his speech reflected a moment ago. Inside the room, this time they're sure they heard a knock that sounds as if it comes from their other room across the upper level hall. Three faces turn toward the sound's source. Baker is naked. Mrs. Baker is locked onto his back (and also naked). And she's buttressed by Tabarnac (still in, and only in, his long black riding coat). They are all in the roaring hot tub.

"Get off me! I forgot Jesse Rod was comin' by…", Baker orders. The three scramble to gather some sort of decorum. First, some quick toweling down and then throwing on a few clothes. Tabarnac remains in his coat but has the decency to fasten the front. He has also left certain areas untowelled in order to savor the flavor later. He has rather thin bony legs that don't fit with his vicious countenance. His Rasputin-like upper parts are now balanced by the comical appearance of his bare bony legs casually crossed as he sits on a sofa. Mrs. Baker ushers in Jesse,

"Come in, Mr. Roid, I'm sorry, Mr. Rod. How are you? Praise be…"

"Great. God bless you, ma'am."

"Mr. Rod! Praise God!…Hey, that rhymes!" Baker exclaims to his own delight. "Praise God for you and yours Mr. Baker. If you hadn't taken my call that night I might've been dead from thinking I was mad…what with seeing Jesus and all. But…just talking to you helped. And then…when you sent those people to help me…well, it just changed my life."

"Thank you, son. Jesus is just that way."

"You ever see Him?"

"Oh, Lordy, We talk all the time. But this time is different. Oh, have you met our associate, Mr. Tabarnac?"

Jesse nods in his direction. He isn't drawn to shake his hand and Tabarnac does not offer his. Tabarnac reminds Jesse of too many people he met while on the street; the kind that will slit your throat for a nickel snack of crack.

"Like I was saying, Mr. Rod…this experience of yours seems a little different. Did Jesus say anything to you?"

"No sir. It was just a very clear vision of the face of Jesus."

"So, no message was delivered at all?" he says suppressing an inner smugness.

"No, sir."

"But clearly, I would have to say, that Jesus must have led you to me, just as he led me here…"

"Yes sir. I think that's true."

"Son, I'd like you to join me on stage at the tent next time…"

"What do you want me to do?" Rod says timidly.

"Just briefly recount that night and how you were led to that TV store and to call me."

"Sir, I'm not a public speaker."

"Son, we'll be with you and God will be with you."

"Well…I'll give it a try." Jesse replies with brave resignation.

"That's all I can ask. God never gives us more than we can handle."

"Yes, sir. Pretty close, though."

Jesse leaves the room and Tabarnac demands,

"OK, back in the tub. Just you two this time. I want to watch." Tabarnac begins loosening his fastenings so that he can finish what they started.

Just then, there's another knock on the door. Out in the hallway, Jesse swears that he hears someone yell, 'God damn it!' Intimidated, he turns to leave. The door opens and Tabarnac is glaring at him from a crack in the door as the greasy visage holds the front of his great coat shut over a tiny bulge.

"I'm sorry. I just wanted to know what time to be there."

From deeper inside the room, over the rushing water. Baker says, "…four…o'…clock."

***

Back at the dealership, Michael has gone out to the dingy smoking area. Outside, the sun is shining. Inside, everybody's bitching. George Suffian is complaining that he only made three grand on his most recent deal. Dave Nelson is upset that his fiance' found out about his girlfriend. Santos is fuming that he'll blow another Sunday helping out at yet another church festival,

"There's too God damn many saints, I tell you. Who can keep them all straight? Hell, now they even say St. Christopher never existed. Did any of them? Or are all of them just made up? Maybe they were just Vatican whores…Hell, I don't know."

Dave Nelson asks, "Which saint is it this time?"

"Oh, I don't know…St. Nektarios of something, I think."

Michael offers,

"That sounds like a good saint for the fruits of summer…" Michael isn't catholic or Greek Orthodox; but it seems strange to demean the saints of one's own church. Why even go?

"Fuck you, new guy. Sold any cars yet…you piece of shit?" Santos grumbles. Michael isn't one for stereotypes; but car salesmen, as a rule, seem to try their best to live up to their reputation. Dave Nelson (who does have a streak of niceness in him) says,

"Your ex going to be there, Santos?"

"No, you piece of crap."

Bobinsky butts in, "You gonna get drunk and try to fuck her…like the Christmas party?"

"Fuck you, you shaggy bitch." This rough language just rolls off the backs of these 'gator-skinned pros. But Michael can make no sense of it. There is none. It's stupid and childish. He's got to get out of here. Before he escapes, everyone realizes that Bobinsky's butting in was just another excuse to drop a trademark in the midst of the group. They all scatter to avoid its effects and Santos shouts after her,

"Look at your ass! You gotta wash your ass!" Paula turns and grins and says,

"My doctor says, 'my asshole'."

Michael finds his refuge in the sun, out back, by the big oak. Suffian has run there, too.

"Hey, George. Wanta get that taste out of your mouth…how 'bout a piece of BibleGum?"

"What is *that*?" George says thinking it must be a joke.

"I got it at Rev. Baker's tent sale the other day. It's pretty good."

"Yes. Give me some. You know those people looked really familiar."

"Who? You mean Baker?"

"Yes. But especially Mrs. Baker. I swear she looks just like this TV personality I used to see in San Francisco."

"What, you mean she used to be a newscaster or something...?"

"No, silly. A TV...a transvestite performer in North Beach...hmmm...is that why they call that area in Miami-South Beach?" George trails off in his afterthought.

"A transvestite dancer? You sure?"

"Well...the years haven't been kind...and the wigs have gotten worse. But 'she' used to bill herself as 'Salome'. We called her 'Salome the salami.'"

"Get out. Salome the salami...(and then in his best Woody Allen) hiding the old salami, eh?"

"Yeah, Pretty tasty, too. Just like this gum. Um, um...Gerbilicious!"

The old plaza, near the downtown bridge to the beach, is a picturesque town square in the Spanish tradition. Other cultures are evident also. There is a band shell from an earlier America. There are cannons from the Spanish and English occupations. There are monuments to fallen vets from the civil war on and many plaques denoting various milestones and incidents in the town's history. Walkways ring the square and bi-sect and criss-cross it. In the summer the band shell still serves to entertain folks. The musical fare is usually so small town typical that Michael has never, intentionally, attended. The plaza is bordered by the bridge on the east, an old Catholic church on the north, a Woolworth's and the Brew House on the south and, in the direction of the Casa Maria, the Spanish Governor's House. It is from this last direction that the unholy trinity of the Bakers and Tabarnac now issue. Michael wishes he had known that today is one of those concert days. The band shell of the plaza, where all have agreed to meet, is being set up for some sort of entertainment.

"Mr. Wade, you're a cameraman now?"

"Just helping out a new friend. Mr. Baker, Mrs. Baker, this is Mary Diana with 20/20."

"Yes. I know. My associate, Mr. Tabarnac here, informed me of your true identity. Just who did you think you were fooling the other day, young lady? You should be ashamed." Mary has to bite her tongue; she needs this interview.

"I'm sorry, Rev. Baker. I wanted to meet you and I didn't want to get Mr. Wade in any trouble. I apologize. Now, where would you like to conduct this interview?"

"I'd like to wait a few minutes until some more people congregate. I want an audience."

"This will air on our next show. That's a national audience. Is that big enough for you?"

"Certainly. 'Course international would be better, heh, heh."

Michael thinks, 'How'd interplanetary be?!" as he contemplates a roundhouse to Baker's chin. Mary diplomatically retorts,

"How about we go over there by the edge of the plaza and shoot you with the bridge at your back? People will see the camera and lights and be drawn to you like flies to…like moths to a flame."

"All right, missy. That's a good compromise. I heard you were good."

As they set up, with Baker as the focus, Mrs. Baker's discreetly by his side and Tabarnac moves well out of camera range. Michael notices that it appears to be a country band setting up as Mary begins,

"We're here tonight with the Rev. TG Baker and his wife, Elisha. We're in the north Florida town of San Jacinto where an unusual phenomenon has occurred. A few weeks ago, a man named Jesse Rod claims to have seen the face of Jesus in the clouds above the cross near the Fountain of Youth attraction. Rev. Baker, how did you happen to come to San Jacinto?"

"That fateful night when Jesse Rod was visited by our Saviour; God led him to a storefront that had my nationally syndicated show, out of Lordstown, Ohio, shining from a big screen TV. Jesse wasn't sure what to do with his vision until God led him to me. Jesse called me right then. I took his call, right there on live TV. I healed him right through the telephone wires. Holy Ghost Power reached right out and shook the devil out of him and stirred his soul. I knew he needed help; so I sent some of my flock to clothe him and care for him. I have been given a vision myself that Jesus will appear very soon…at the cross…with a new message…for a new age."

"I've noticed that you haven't asked for offerings at your gatherings here. What's the reason for that?"

"Jesus has specifically told me to *not* ask for prayer offerings at this glorious occasion."

Mary decides to delay delving into Baker's statement that Jesus 'told' him and pursues her planned progression of probes,

"How much money did you make with your ministry last year?"

"I believe that's between me and the Lord."

"And the IRS?"

"Render unto Caesar what is Caesars. I have no problems with the infernal revenooers. My organization is tax exempt."

"I have seen documents where you claimed personal wealth of over twenty million dollars. Do you deny this?"

"I don't know where you got your information, little lady…but the bulk of what I have is held in trust for the eventual building of the World International Charismatic Christian Assembly complex that will house offices, Christian condominiums and a Bible Land Theme Park for all the young Christian boys and girls to enjoy. Matter of fact…I'm considering building it right here…out near Nine Mile Pass…next to the newly erected Golf Association for Seniors on some land owned by a local Christian businessman."

"Do you believe that taking such a vast amount of money from those that turn to you for help is sanctioned by God?"

"All I know is this…people give to me voluntarily. They give what they wish. God has never told me to not accept love offerings…except for right now…and right here…and that's what I'm doing."

"Is it true that you met your wife in San Francisco?" Baker seems startled,

"…Yes. Why?"

"Could you tell me the circumstances of how you met?"

"I'll tell you it was many years ago and it's none of your da…, uh-business."

"Mrs. Baker, would you care to elaborate on that?" Elisha senses Mary knows something but bets she couldn't possibly know the whole truth,

"I'm not proud; but I'm not ashamed to admit that I've sinned in the past. That…is what this man is all about…showing people the way out."

"If you must know, little lady, I met Elisha back in the Haight-Ashbury during the early days of my ministry. I saved her, she saved me and God saved us both. Praise His holy name."

"Did you also meet Mr. Tabarnac there?"

"Well…yes."

"And what is his relationship to you?"

"Business advisor, confidante, friend."

"What has Jesus told you will happen when he appears?"

"Only that He will appear and here will deliver His new message to the world."

"And he has spoken directly to you?"

"Just as clear as His crown of thorns." Mary's not thrilled with this interview; but brings it to a close,

"Thank you Rev. and Mrs. Baker." As Mary turns to do her close; the band shell erupts with a hot country fiddle tearing into Charlie Daniels 'The Devil Went Down to Georgia' causing Michael to think, 'Georgia's only 50 miles away…' Mary recaptures his attention with,

"Hey cameraman. Aim that thing this way, will you?"

"Yes, ma'am."

"This is Mary Diana. We'll have more on this story later."

The Baker troupe starts wandering toward the band shell. As they near it, they are met by a tall middle-aged southern gentleman type with thick white hair. He's wearing a dark blue pin stripe suit.

"Mary...that guy's familiar...That's one of our state senators, Sanford Mims."

"I guess things are heating up if the politicians are getting involved."

"Mary. Let's go up to the veranda of the Brew House and see what goes on from there." They make their way to the second level of the watering hole; this time seating themselves toward the side over looking the plaza. They are surprised to see Senator Mims take the stage after the band finishes their opening number. They're unable to make out every word clearly from their seats; but, apparently, Mims is introducing Baker. Indeed, Baker mounts the stage and begins another diatribe.

"Frankly, I'm glad we can't hear him. He pisses me off." Michael says bitterly.

"Unfortunately, it's my job to hear everything I can. Damn. I couldn't shake him loose today. My questions went nowhere..."

"Just think of it as a preliminary round...Round one...that's all."

"Yes. But sometimes you don't get another shot."

"You can still do a lot of digging. Face it...you just didn't have much to go on today except that Baker's an asshole...selling salvation. The real story here is Jesus."

"Yes. But I haven't met him."

"Me neither. Do you believe in Jesus?"

"Honestly...I don't know...Even though I was raised Catholic; it was more of a rehearsed ritual than anything else. I've always believed in doing the right thing. *That's* been my religion. I've always felt there is a 'higher power'...a God. But...I've had to grope for any true answers. When I was pretty young..."

"Pretty *and* young, I bet." Michael inserts as Mary continues her thought,

"I went to our parish priest...in Newark...and asked him, 'What do you think God wants me to do?'"...Do you know...what he said? He said, 'Maybe you should be a secretary.' I said, '**No**, what does God want us all to do?' His face went blank...He had no answer...Oh, the painful price we pay for priestly paralysis." This last phrase causes Michael to almost gag on his drink, which has recently arrived.

"Priestly paralysis?...I've got to remember that one...Say, do you believe in heaven...or hell?"

"You mean it's a choice? Nah, just kidding...Actually, I've always loved the depiction of heaven. It looks so beautiful...Hell, I've just never put much credence in it."

"I think God is merciful. Otherwise, how could there be so many assholes in the world?...I think we're given many clues...and many chances. I even think it's so simple that the answer eludes us. I think we should constantly listen to our inner selves. I believe that we can guide ourselves through this life-maze by, first, believing in the Goodness and Greatness of God; then...extending that...into all areas of our life. A sort of constant prayer of thanks...In the Methodist services...they have a beautiful affirmation...that is sung. It begins (here Michael's voice becomes melodic and strong) 'Praise God from whom all blessings flow' (it reminds Mary of a Gregorian chant). But...I had to change some of the words."

"Why?" Mary says giggling.

"Because...I don't believe God is *just* a man and it's really presumptuous of us to think that God looks human *at all*. Lately, I'm thinking I may change some other words..."

"You didn't use the word 'man.'"

"The rest of the original words go (here Michael only speaks the words) 'Praise *Him* all creatures here below. Praise *Him* above ye heavenly hosts. Praise *Father, Son* and Holy Ghost.' The way I do it now is this (here he 'sings' again):

'Praise God from whom all blessings flow
Praise God all creatures here below
Praise God above ye heavenly hosts
Praise Father, Mother, Holy Ghost."

"What would you change now?"

"Well, I really don't believe in the trinity. In my mind God is all three. Feminine, masculine and ethereal. Not three parts; but many aspects of one part."

"Let's sing it together."

"Really?" Michael says as excitedly as a little kid at his own birthday party.

"I'll follow just behind you."

"OK, here goes…"

Scattered patrons look around as the duo begin their singsong. Simultaneously, varied caterwauled paeans to Bakers preaching talents spew from the town square. The resulting duet (with choral backing) looks something like this;

Praise God from whom all blessings flow
Praise God!   *Death to abortionists!*
Praise God all creatures here below
Hallelujah, Brother!   *Bless you, TG, bless you*
Praise God above ye heavenly hosts
Holy Ghost Power!   *Holy Ghost power!*
Praise Father, Mother, Holy Ghost

Michael's line of sight on this last line includes:

Baker, Elisha, Tabarnac.

The Brew House patrons may have seen:

Michael, Mary Diana, Skates

(As he stood near the door to take a peek).

"Tabarnac!!", yells Baker after descending the band shell steps. "Tabarnac, come here!! Let's go back to the room and figure out what to do about that little bitch, Mary."

Michael and Mary watch as their 'song' ends and the rival cheering section fades and Baker's group moves towards the Casa Maria. They look at each other softly; unaware that they had been vocal competition with Baker's crowd. Michael asks,

"Did you feel anything physical from that chant? You know…there are those that say the monks that developed the liturgical chants did them one note at a time…writing down the note only when it moved through them…of the Spirit. Still others believe that chants, all sound, open or affect various centers, chakras, within the body. Sound can affect us greatly. Remember…that's one reason I became attracted to you…your voice. So…did you feel any centers open in your body?"

She puts her hand just to the left of the center of her chest and says,

"Just about here, I think…"

After a brief pause, Michael reaches over and takes her hand and says, softly,

"Good. That's good."

"Michael, why don't we finish these drinks and go up to the room and check out the tape?"

When the drinks are downed; Mary and Michael withdraw to the Casa Maria. Mary pops in the tape of Baker's interview. She still isn't pleased with it. Michael's camera work is fine, she just didn't get any insight into Baker or his plans. She doesn't want to besmirch Baker's wife on the word of one car salesman. And putting people down really isn't her forte; her strength lies in opening people up so that they reveal their own truths. She opens a discourse by saying,

"Michael, when this airs I'll probably help get Baker more exposure than he's ever gotten before. I've got to find out more…to piece togeth-er…before this gets on."

"Well, you can edit it; can't you?"

"Yes, but I really don't like his guy *and* his unholy trinity…"

"Did you know the word 'trinity' appears nowhere in the bible?"

"No", she says dismissively. "But I really don't want to contribute to helping Baker get an audience."

"Mary…Listen…The story isn't Baker…It's Jesus. More important-ly; it's God. Focus on God. *You* can deliver a message from God! That's the story!"

"You're right. I'm being diverted by Baker. (She softens.) You know… you center me. That's a nice feeling. I was about to get really bugged. Thanks."

"You excite me…I really needed to know why I was here in this small, strange, foreign town. Now…I know. There will be a message of great importance delivered here…and…I've found a woman worthy of Love."

"Let's not use the 'L' word yet, OK? Let's just see where we go", she cautions. Mary leans closer to Michael as she turns to him. Michael slides over a bit on the couch where they're sitting and, after a brief mental hesitation, they are pulled gently into a kiss.

Mary's lifestyle of working on the road has her in a mood for tearing off clothes and getting a good wild fuck. The softness of Michael's kiss surprises her. He is so sincere. It's like a kiss of thankfulness; grateful-ness; that he's been granted this opportunity. He can't help it. He could no more grab her right now, as if she was just any woman, than a rope could pass through the eye of a needle. To Mary, this kiss feels better than any penis that has ever been inside her. She has been involved with rich and powerful men as well as a few hunks. This is different. She inwardly shudders to think, 'Is this the first time I've ever felt Love? Is that possible?' She can feel her body yield, willingly, to Michael's touch. Her skin seems so sensitive. She feels a quim; a quiver. Leading her to quickly ponder, 'Is a quim akin to a quiver? As long as it's in the right place.' They move to the bed in a rhythmic harmony that feels very unawkward…so the arrow may find its way. The room is brightly lit; but Michael sees only Mary in his mind. His eyes are shut. Not to close out the beauty there; but to *feel* the true expanse of beauty with his inner eye. His hand finds her engorged organ and he pulls on it slightly; running two fingers on either side and then folding her loose labia over it. This, to him, is a declaration. If she wants him; he's ready to be hers. Somehow, he thinks, this can work. Foreplay is shortened, as this isn't so much sex, as Love. He doesn't think about pleasing himself or her. He doesn't worry about pre-maturely coming. This is a union; in the highest human sense. He enters her…and his body is no longer his; but theirs. In his mind's eye he sees (feels?) a blue light circling. The shape is very similar to the yin-yang symbol ☯; only the light keeps exploding on the outer rim. It reminds him of the powerful remnants of creation still forming and erupting at the edges of the universe. Images long imagined and now confirmed as reality as they're beamed to us via the Hubble telescope. Two in one. Two becoming one. Two having found one. Mary's breath is in small gulps as her heart takes off. It almost overwhelms her. For a moment she thinks she may stop breathing altogether. Michael senses this and strokes her in a calming, assuring manner. She knows this is real. Thoughts quickly flicker through her mind, "Will this be enough?…Do I want this *now*?' Those thoughts soon disappear as she realizes, 'Yes, I do want this. Yes! I've always wanted this.'

After a time; there is a mutual unspoken signal that something's got to come,er-give, that is. Michael doesn't want to, he just wants to stay inside her forever. But her body is at the point of no return and Michael wants her to be there. Soon Mary's fluids squirt from her inner walls and Michael feels the warmness. He returns the compliment…and yin and yang mix and meld and mesh to-get-her. They lay side by side. Michael's right leg is thrust between her legs; his penis still in her. As they hug in exhaustion; they peacefully drift off…unaware that,a few floors above, Baker and company are discussing them and how to deal with this nosy reporter.

"Tabarnac, what are we going to do about that girl?" Baker ejaculates as Elisha interjects,

"I think any publicity is good publicity."

"Now deary. That may be true in Hollywood; but not Lordstown. Tabarnac?"

"Of course, my natural predilection is for killing her. But that may be pre-mature. Perhaps your dear wife is correct. You, my friend, have the gift of language that can turn people to your way. If this woman's report draws people to this nauseating little town; it will only mean your audience will be bigger, no?"

"Well, yes, no. I guess so…"

"Do you think you are deluded?"

"Good God, no. This happened…You ever seen me *not* collect money?"

"No. But…we do have that little arrangement with Harrison, qui?"

"Yes. And if all goes right; we'll have our little Christian village, too." Baker chortles as Tabarnac openly ponders,

"That 'messenger', of the house of Rod, he bothers me", says Tabarnac as Elisha submits,

"Yes, lordy, no tellin' what he saw or heard the other day. Should we just keep an eye on him, honey?"

"Yes, for right now…He's our pipeline to heaven. He's going to be our drawing card."

Mary and Michael are startled from their reverie as the phone rings in the room. Mary instinctively jerks toward the phone thus pulling Michael from his final resting place inside her as she groggily garbles her greeting,

"Hello, Mary Diana here…"

"Hello, this is Father Leonard, I hope it's not too late to be calling…"

"No Father. I had…I had just fallen asleep. How can I help you?" (damn-it had to be a priest)

Michael stumbles out on the other side of the bed and makes his way to the bathroom while half trying to hide his still erect member as it is now swollen from liquid accumulation. Mary notices and gives a thumbs up sign thinking. 'Wow, he's still hard.'

"Mary, I thought you'd be interested to know that the monsignor in Jacksonville just called to tell me that the Church is sending someone to take a closer look at our little town. It's all very unofficial. But to me it's significant."

"Do you know the person they are sending?"

"Yes, but not well. He's quite a well-known religious scholar; Father Ben Asher. He's arriving tomorrow. I thought it might help your story and that your story might help the Church."

"Father, that's very thoughtful of you. Thank you. Do you think you could arrange for us to meet?"

"I'll have to ask him; but I'm sure that will be fine. May I call you tomorrow after I've spoken with him?"

"Just leave a message here and the hotel will reach me. And Father,thanks."

"You're welcome."

Michael exits the chamber as Mary rises to greet him from their nap with a hug. For just a moment she wants to withdraw thinking, "Isn't this when they decide they've had enough?' It's too late; Michael envelops her in his arms. He's happy. He has no problem letting her know as he paraphrases Dr. King.

"I have been to the mountaintop. And I'm glad you came there with me."

"My pleasure…our pleasure", she concedes.

"Mary; my boy has only recently begun living with me. I had no idea this would happen tonight…though I was hopeful it would happen… sometime. I'd better call him."

"Look, Michael, it's early enough that it won't look funny if you just go now", she says still expecting him to be like all the rest.

"Sure you don't mind? I'd like to prepare him if I won't be there."

"No, I understand."

Michael isn't certain, but he, almost unbelievingly, detects her very recent Love beginning to withdraw into a protective shell. He places his hands firmly on her two shoulders and looks her in the eye,

"Mary…what you felt from me is real. Do not doubt it."

He says this so straightforwardly that, inside, she can feel the truth of his words. She will still be cautious.

"Call me later…OK?…Michael…"

"You couldn't keep me from it" he smiles and hugs her good-bye.

Michael thinks about *something* almost all the time (Don't we all?) Right now, as he lazily steers his car homeward; he's thinking about Love. All of his life, it seems, he's been consumed with the idea of finding the ideal mate. Looking, seeking, searching. His obsession has led to some very bad decisions. He'd been with a high number of women. All for a very short time. The most recent, before his move to San Jac, had devastated him. Just to recall her 'attributes' caused his mind to reel. She was the daughter of an abusive mom (a trait she'd inherited). Her father was an alcoholic, high-ranking government official. She was bi-sexual (in a selfish sort of way). She had worked for years as an out-call masseuse (a euphemism for prostitute [one of her favorite jokes went-'How do you make a hormone? Don't pay her'…rim shot, please]). And, to top it off (and explain her temper), her birthday was the same as Hitler. Michael had been attracted to her spirit? She had steeled his. Never again would he look at women the same way. For a while he became an unwitting misogynist. That passed. He had always been fascinated with women. In his younger years he would look at *any* woman he thought held a glimmer of hope of being in his future; imagining that woman as wife, mother, growing old together-all this in a matter of seconds upon first fantasizing over someone. Over the years, he'd even developed a system of evaluating their unseen parts by equating breasts with the shape of the nose and lower openings with the shape of the mouth. Since this great scientific work was based on extensive research and not mere supposition; it was remarkably accurate. In case equally scientific means were being used on him; he always wore his shoes a half-size too big.

With all his haphazard Love explorations, one wouldn't expect it; but he truly believed in monogamy. Youthful urges often won out. But as he grew and began to realize you don't get 'til you give and that ones word is paramount in this life; he really determined to be faithful to the woman of the moment even if that faith wasn't returned. He now knows that he could be faithful. It just wasn't worth it for him to experience one more body without a soul. He wanted the whole package. He now knew, that with good faith, he could bend and adjust to any relationship that was honest and would lead to a higher form of union.

As he pulls up to his cottage he has a peaceful, playful half-smile on his face. He goes in and finds Skates in the living room waiting to rib his Dad,

"Hey, Dad. I heard your 'performance' at the Brew House…Getting chummy with Mary,huh-Dad, huh-are ya?"

"Yes, sir. Pretty neat lady there. I hope to be spending some time with her."

"Gettin' serious, eh?"

"Yeah…actually; I am. I think she's a little freaked. But…I like her. How's your life?"

"Good. I'm tired though. Just going to hang and watch some TV."

"I'm going to give Mary a call. See you in a minute."

Michael goes to his room to dial Mary at the hotel,

"Hey. Watcha' doin'?"

"I started focusing…like you said. Listen to this. I want to have an on-air roundtable discussion with representatives of several major religions to get their faith's views on the possible re-appearance of Jesus. What do you think?"

"Cool. Great idea. I know this rabbi in town that seems like a nice intelligent man…You could get that guy that Leonard said was coming in…Hey…where's the Dalai Lama?"

As Michael comes out to say goodnight; the phone rings. Skates answers and, after some hushed, hurried talking, announces that he's got to go out for a while.

"Skates. It's after 10…you've got school tomorrow. Don't be too late. OK?"

"Don't worry. Dad. It's important."

Sub 5-1
Michael's Jesus

Michael is alone in his room. Lying down. Reflecting on the day, his life, his son and his desire to Love. The ceiling fan whirs a whisper of a breeze across his body in the darkened room. It feels cool on his skin; a soft, gentle feeling. An unexpected subtle sense of another presence in the room causes Michael to sit up. It's a mere sensation of a presence. This isn't a new feeling; but rare. And special. What is the message to be this time, he thinks, as he waits for the presence to deliver. There. Now he can feel it. Now it is solidifying. A benign, barely perceptible mani-festation settles at the foot of the bed. Michael tries to relax into it. To receive as much as possible. He feels there is nothing to fear. There it is. Clearer. Jesus. Gentle Jesus. Raiment of white robes. His just shoulder length hair pushed back slightly as if the fan's fluttering is effecting it. 'This is pretty real…' Michael thinks 'Jesus, his hair is moving…'. The vision is almost physical as gentle eyes look deeply into Michael,

"Michael. Soon…I will appear…and then…I will disappear."

"What do you mean?…was Baker right?"

"He only knows that I will be there…to you I am giving my message."

"Why me, Lord?"

"Please, call me Jesus."

"Yes, sir."

"Call me Jesus."

"Yes, si-uh-Jesus."

"Because you have already accepted what it is I will say…because your life, though lived in private, is known to me…because your life is the pursuit of Love. That was my message all along…Now…I'm tired. I must rest…Too many call on me…They must learn…that I am only a key…Not the lock and not the door."

"Did you appear to Baker, too?"

"Yes."

"Why have you no crown of thorns now?"

"It hurts." The answer causes Michael to laugh; but he stops himself. *Should* he laugh?

"You can laugh. *All* should learn to laugh…But seriously, folks-no-just kidding…I appeared to Baker in pain and suffering because that is how he makes me feel. All those that call on me everyday keep me in bondage…My message will be this…Believe in God…Believe that God is in all things; seen and unseen…God is all. God is all of us. All of you. God is in the rocks and weeds. God is in the void in your lives. This alone…must be your understanding. You, alone, are your own saviour. This is my message. God rules all. You may lift your voices in praise and thanks; but no longer must man call down heaven. Rather, raise up your Spirit to meet it."

"Wow. But what am I to do with this knowledge?"

"Be a witness. Tell my message. Not beyond your own capacity. By being there…you will help to disseminate this new knowledge. I ask your help."

"Willingly, gladly." A grateful Michael accepts as the image fades and he slips into slumber.

"What...what's...' the sound of an intrusive telephone startles Michael from peaceful dreams. As he sleepily, swiftly pulls the phone from cradle to ear; he hears,

"Marsilius Sandile...that's who you're looking for..." A squint at the nightstand clock tells him it's approaching midnight,

"Who is this?...Whitey?", Michael says to the voice on the other end.

"Marsilius Sandile...He's the guy with the red mark on his tire."

"Where can I find him?...How did *you* find him?", Michael assumes he's talking to Whitey and, from the boisterous background, that Whitey's calling from the Rib Station.

"Your son came wheelin' in here about an hour ago...said he spotted a kid on a bike with a red tire mark. He took me down to Central and pointed him out...a couple of questions to the right people and I had his name and address."

Michael's thinking, 'Now what do I do?' All he really wants to do is talk to the kid. How can he orchestrate a controlled situation where no one gets hurt? What words could he possibly say that will get this kid to listen? Can he pull this off without getting arrested for kidnapping...or something?

"Whitey...I've got zero experience...to even know how to approach, much less resolve, something like this...Do you have any ideas?"

"Well...we'd have to keep it private; discreet-like, you know...Hold on...Your son wants to speak to you."

"Dad...This guy can be had. A friend of mine cops from him sometimes..."

"Cops what?"

"Dad...you don't want to know...But it's nothing I do. Can we leave it at that?Wait...wait a minute...Whitey's got an idea. Here he is."

"Look, Michael. Let's not put Skates in the middle of this..."

"Hell, no."

"But…he did give me an idea. There's an old-timer…strums down here once in a while…good man…occasionally does a little blow. I think I can persuade him to help you set this fellow up…"

"Like…how?"

"Let me call you tomorrow."

"OK…Remember…he's got a gun! And tell Skates to get home, will ya?!"

Somewhere in dreamtime, Michael has decided to throw a cook-out…at his house. Under the big oak at Cadillac the next day; Michael approaches Whitey. Whitey is the only person at Cadillac he cares to invite.

"Hey, Whitey. What's up?"

"Not much. What you got?"

"A little ginger chicken mixed with some leftover veggies-you?"

"A sea-bass sandwich."

"Sounds great. Say. Speaking of food, as we always do, how'd you and Mary Rose like to come over to my place Sunday afternoon for a cookout. I'm not going to call it a bar-b-que; because that's your realm. I was thinking…maybe…steaks and shrimp…for the carnivorously challenged. Or is that carnally challenged?…"

"Depends on what mood you're in…(Whitey deadpans and then goes on) No-seriously…it sounds great…Who else is coming to dinner?"

"Oh, maybe George and Nicholas and JR and…(Michael can see Whitey starting to re-consider) No, no. Just joking. Me and Mary Diana, my son and his girlfriend and you and Mary Rose. Small group."

"OK then. As long as you've revised your guess list; we'll be there…I'll bring the Red Stripe."

"About 2 o'clock: OK?"

"Sounds good."

"Say, Whitey…what did you find out about the 'hyena'?"

"Hyena?…Oh, you mean Sandile. I set it up for tonight…at the Rib Station. I'll fill you in later. Right now…let's eat."

After lunch, Michael makes a couple more calls to confirm his other dinner guests. While inviting Mary Diana, she asks if he can get in touch with the rabbi he mentioned and to see if there are representatives of Islam and Buddhism present in this small town. He remembers seeing a small white building on 207, out near 95, that said something about Islam on its sign. He finds the number in the yellow pages and leaves a message. He has less luck locating Buddhists, so he tries the Jacksonville book. There he finds a listing for the Tibetan Buddhist Temple and reaches a young sounding monk named Tenzin Gyatso who would be happy to participate in any religious discussion. Next, the rabbi-'What was his name?' He goes in search of George Suffian who originally introduced Michael to him. George is in his cube making calls.

"Hey, George. What was the name of that rabbi customer of yours?"

"Neil?"

"Yeah, that's him. I couldn't remember his name. Can I have his number to see if he'll agree to be on a religious panel to discuss the sightings at the church?"

"I suppose so. But don't you try to get him to buy a car, you hear?!"

"Wouldn't think of it."

"You're getting pretty chummy with those TV people, aren't you?"

"One in particular." Michael answers as George writes down the requested number. Michael turns to his desk to dial.

"Hi. This is Michael Wade from Cadillac. I'm trying to reach Rabbi Tzedakah. Is he there?" The female on the other end goes to get him. Once the rabbi is on the line; he, also, is agreeable to being on the panel. 'Good. Now only the Islamic reps haven't been reached.' Michael wonders, "Who will represent the Protestants? Maybe they shouldn't be represented...this is all happening on Catholic land.' His next thought almost gives him literal chills, 'Oh, God...I hope Mary doesn't want Rev. Baker...what a horrible spokesman for Protestantism.'

Sub 5-2
Hyena II Dos

The old man sits on a stump, strumming a light blues riff in the dark…out back of Whitey's place, next to the ramshackle lean-to wood shed. His deep brown skin is accented by his almost true black high set cheekbones reflecting the lone light coming from the back door of the rib joint. From a bushy area beside the building, a thin youth, with an 'S' on his baseball cap pulled tight around his face, emerges. In a shouted whisper, the youth derisively declares,

"Old man. I got your shit."

"Hush, boy. This ain't no R.O.C. cola you're bringin' me. Come on in here", the old man says motioning towards the door of the woodshed. He creaks open the door and…its even darker inside. The youth rushes past the old man to enter the shed as he turns back and says,

"Hurry up, old man. It ain't like this deal's gonna make me rich." Suddenly, the old man shoves the youth hard through the doorway and several bodies slam the brash youth, thief to the ground. He feels a knee on his chest pinning him to the earthen floor. A large hand is on his throat and two other sets of hands secure his legs. He's wiry and has survival adrenaline pumping through his veins. His right arm is trying to wriggle something from the waistband underneath his oversized shirt. Just then the powerful blast of a Q-Beam hunting light blinds him until he can make out the image of a gun barrel point-blank on the tip of his nose.

"OK, OK-whatdaya want; let me up, godamit!"

"Shut up! Shut up right now", Michael says cocking the hammer on his pistol. The youth stops struggling and stops talking.

"Whitey, get his gun."

Whitey lifts the shirt and finds not a gun, but an eight-inch piece of metal stuffed in the boy's pants. Whitey observes,

"Well, sometimes you just don't need a gun…now do ya? If it's dark enough you can simply scare the shit out of people…with this, can't ya boy…"

The youth doesn't respond, so Michael makes a cursory body pat on the kid and finds no other weapon; then says,

"Now, are you Marsilius Sandile?"

"Wazittoya?"

"You dumb fuck…You don't even know when people are trying to help you, do ya?" Michael isn't quite sure how to proceed from here. Perceiving this; Whitey suggests,

"Turn him over. Since he isn't ready to co-operate, let me tie his hands behind his back. Skates, get his feet. (After he's trussed; Whitey orders-) Isaiah, help me set him up on that woodpile. Turn on the shed light. And Michael-turn off that damn Q-Beam. It's going to blind us all."

The hog-tying is done and the one dim bulb dangling from a cord overhead replaces the blinding Q-Beam. They move Marsilius to a corner away from the lone window and door and Michael begins,

"Now just sit there. I want to talk to you. Do you remember 'seeing the light' on another recent night?"

"What are you talking about?" Marsilius is settling down a bit; but still has too much attitude to listen. Michael's pissed. And determined to get his attention. He's already pumped from his own adrenaline rush. It's not like this is an everyday occurrence for him. Matter of fact; it's a neverday occurrence for him. He's starting to shake with rage. He grabs the Q-Beam again and flicks it on right in the hyena's eyes. It's all he can do to not grab this little terd and shake him to pieces,

"Now, listen, you little piece of shit. Stop! Stop right now! I'm a peaceful man. But right now I could blow you away and dump you in a 'gator filled swamp and never look back. (He grabs the collar of the offender and almost squeezes the handle off the light; holding himself from thrusting the hot light directly into the face he's so close to.) Now…are you going to LISTEN!"

"All right, all right", and Marsilius slumps into subservience.

"What do you want, white man?"

"That's just it. You think it's all black and white. Well, it isn't. You held me up the other night. You freaked me out. You pissed me off. And you scared me. Then you fuckin' hit me. All for 20 bucks. Was that twenty worth it?"

Flippantly, Marsilius answers,

"Well, it seemed like it then…"

Michael is boiling inside; but he knows he can't let it show any more than it already has. He's always been afraid of losing his temper. He believes he could kill. He must not become more violent. He's trying not to lose sight of his perceived mission here. If he's to teach this young thief anything; he must rise above feelings of revenge or deadly anger. This…is a teaching mission. He adjusts his tone,

"Mar-sil-i-us…", he says slowly, mockingly, "I have seen a man with a 45 caliber hole in his chest…over a 50 cent sandwich. I once saw a man blown away in Mexico…for a cigarette. Worth, maybe a penny…" The word 'penny' trails off and bends down as if the copper piece of which he speaks is falling to the ground. "I have no idea what you are, how you were raised, if you have any heroes worth following. I don't know. But…I'm telling you one thing tonight. You will not steal from anyone in this neighborhood again. I live here…and I ain't movin'. Now. We have, in this little room tonight, members of the Black community and members of the White community. We have Mr. Whitey Grayer. You probably know him. We have Mr. Isaiah Washington. Son of the minister of the 1st A.M.E. Church down here on Central. From one of the founding families of this area. You may know him, too. And, we've got me and him", he says pointing to Skates, but seeing no reason to name himself nor his son. He motions to Skates,

"Get the camera." Skates produces a Polaroid with flash.

"I hope you take this opportunity to see the light." Michael frames the shot to show the boy's face but not his hands tied behind his back.

He cracks off four shots in rapid succession; once again leaving Marsilius blinking to see.

"I have no idea how many chances you've been given in the past... but...if you perpetrate any further crimes upon any one of any color in this area; you will go immediately to jail. If I even *suspect* that you're the guy doing bad stuff around here, I will turn you in for that crime and swear I saw it. And...I will turn you in as the man that got me the other night. If you try anything on any one of us here, these pictures are going in a special place that will finger you. So you better pray that nothing happens to us...You been to prison yet, Marsilius? Not just jail. I mean prison. Not just 'juvy'. The real thing. Have ya?"

"No, sir", he says with the slightest hint of respect.

"Strong men come out of there with different lips than they went in with. They're rounder; more tubular. Some come out with front teeth smashed in...to make it easier to insert foreign objects. Some come out and have trouble sitting down for a while due to the same foreign objects being inserted. You may be bad right now; but you'll meet some mean, mean people in there; and your sweet, skinny frame will be like ripe meat for them. Sure, you'll get tough again...when you get out. But...you'll never forget. You'll push those thoughts to the back of your head; but they'll never go away. Did you ever meet a really tough guy with a lisp? It's a strange sight. But I've seen it. Weird, man. I've just given you your future. So, you've got two choices. You can leave town and go down any way you want. But...if you stay here, *you will not repeat the things you do now. Do you understand?*"

"Yes, sir."

"Now, how much money you got on you? Whitey, flip his pockets." Whitey turns them inside out and finds,

"33 bucks and a small glassene baggie."

Michael takes twenty bucks and the baggie. He opens the baggie and dumps it's white powdery contents onto the dirt floor of the shed and grinds it into the earth with his shoe.

"What're ya doin', man? I gotta pay for that!"

"I'm takin' the twenty 'cause that's what you stole. I'm takin' the powder 'cause you need a lesson. I'm also takin' your bike and turning it in to the police. I bet it's stolen anyway and some kid is missing it. You work out whatever you have to with your man about the coke. But if I see you on the street late at night hangin' out shufflin' shit; I *will* turn you in. I've got your name; I've got your number; I know who your momma is. Quit fuckin' around. You've been warned."

Michael turns to the younger people to his side and says,

"Go outside and get his bike; then you guys get out of here. Whitey, I'm going to untie this dude; keep him covered. And Marsilius-we're keeping your little 'gun', too." Whitey and Michael escort Marsilius to the door and release him into the night. He quickly slithers away like a lizard let loose.

"What do you think? Did we do any good?", Michael says with a sigh of relief and the faintest hint of a smile.

"Hard to tell. Only slime will tell." They both laugh as the tension lessens and their respective adrenaline returns to wherever it is that adrenaline stays until needed once again.

Citrus Chili Salad

Two heads romaine lettuce, shredded in bowl.

On the side, mix well 1/3rd cup fresh lemon juice, sprinkle of sea salt and ground pepper, ½ cup grapeseed oil and 2 teaspoons chili powder or ground cumin.

Add mix to greens. Toss and serve.

CHAPTER SIX

Testify

"What...you idiot...you did what? You could go to jail...for kidnapping...assault..." Mary's pissed. Michael's wishing he'd have kept this incident to himself, shortly after he's begun relating it to his love in Mary's hotel room later that same night.

"There weren't even any bullets in the gun..."

"That's not the point."

"What is the point?" Michael responds while trying to reel his words back in as soon as they pass the threshold of his lips. He doesn't want to make this argumentative; he realizes she's only saying that she cares. At least he hopes that's her motivation.

"The point is-you committed a crime. That's the point."

"Look. I'm glad you care. But the cops sure weren't going to do anything about a twenty-dollar robbery. And they sure weren't going to care about that kid. I was trying to save his life."

"You could've been hurt...Killed! You didn't know what was going to happen."

"No. I didn't. But haven't you ever done something rash when you thought you might be right?"

"Yes. But I'm a professional."

"You have training in this?" Again, re-sucking his own air. Just sucking.

"Training? They don't teach this. It's experience."

"Mary. Please. Listen. I understand what you're saying. Maybe I shouldn't have told you about this. I respect you enough to not want to keep anything relevant from you. Do you understand this?"

"Yes. I guess so. I shouldn't have reacted. I don't want you to get hurt, that's all...unless...it's with me." She smiles these last few words to

Michael and the edginess of the situation dissipates. Michael moves to her and offers,

"I think you only argue with ass-holes and people you care about. Luckily, this is the latter."

"So. No potentially deadly confrontations…unless we're together. OK?"

"OK."

Sunday afternoon arrives and it's a beautiful one. Michael has the grill set up lakeside. This side of his house has a low stone wall separating his property from the public walkway that circumnavigates the brackish lake. The 'lake' is less than a half-mile end to end; but it adds so much to his home. Being able to look out and see water rippled by a gentle wind, a few year round ducks and geese furiously paddling with webbed feet unseen from the surface. Occasionally, snowy egrets and pelicans grace the shallow waterway, as well. The shoreline, rimmed with trees (mostly pecan, oak and palm) and cute one-story homes on his side and more stately older homes across the way, imparts a feeling of instant peacefulness. The 'lake' is actually an inlet from the bay that has been dammed at one end to stem its ebb and flow and give it a constant level. The small dam is to the right as you look from the house out onto the lake. The left end of the lake gives way to a street leading to the historical center of the town. At one time that street had been water; an extension of the lake. The entire flow from bay to bay had been a stream that once formed the western edge of the ancient city. This is a fine place for friends to gather. Mary Diana is the first to arrive. She peers through the screen door of the kitchen and sees Skates preparing something at the counter. He senses her,

"Mary. Come on in. Dad's out by the lake."

Mary wanders through the house with a big smile and two bottles of Chianti. She feels comfortable here. She reaches the 'front' lakeside door and goes outside,

"Hey, big guy. How are you?"

'Great. Whatcha got there?" Michael says as he embraces her with his elbows so as not to dirty her garments with his charcoal darkened hands.

"Oh, a couple of jugs for the party."

"I was admiring your jugs from afar", he teases.

"Got pretty close the other night", she retorts.

"And…I hope to again."

Michael sees Whitey and Mary Rose peeking through the lakeside door,

"Hey, this where the party is?"

"This *is* the place. Bring yourself on out." Michael beckons and introduces the Marys and Whitey since they've never met formally.

"Guess you can never have too many Marys." Michael chuckles to his guests. Whitey and Mary have brought a cooler of Red Stripe and a sweet potato pie. Inside the house Skates answers a ringing phone. It's his date for the day and she can't make it. While he's telephonically dealing with that disappointment, the call-waiting feature beeps in,

"Dad (he yells through the open bay window), it's some guy from the Islamic Center. Something about 'his ham', I think…" Skates returns to the kitchen to finish his honey glaze for the shrimp barbie while Michael hands off the fire tending duties to Whitey so that he can take the call.

"Michael Wade here." The voice of Islam responds,

"As-Salaam-Alaikum, Mr. Wade, this is Yusef Ibn Hisham. You left a message at the center…" Michael explains the TV panel idea and Yusef accepts, as it will be an opportunity for Islam to be seen on American television in something other than a terrorist light. Michael thanks him and says, "Salaam." He then bounds outside,

"Mary, I think we've got a pretty good panel now. An Islamic scholar, a Buddhist monk that was taught directly by the Dalai Lama, a rabbi, Father Asher and…Are you going to put Baker on the panel?"

"I think I have to...even though...(she says with a guileful smile) it might make you WASPs look bad."

"Yeah, a great representative of my kind", Michael states sarcastically. With all the furor and upheaval occurring in the town and within the lives of those present, it seems natural that a full-blown religious and philosophical discussion will ensue. Michael begins with this assertion,

"I've been spiritual all my life...I've found it impossible not to be. There has always been a vital, discerned presence in my life...something that is in me and beyond me. Something that, if I pay attention and don't color my feelings, will guide me through any situation. I call it God."

"I met a lot of Black Muslims in the navy...they always said that part of their faith...is that each of us has no excuse to dismiss or disavow God because...before time began...God assembled all souls and told us of our bond and duty...", Whitey recounts and Michael acknowledges,

"You know, I can relate to that feeling...Like I was just saying...that 'presence' has always been there...as if it's imprinted on my soul." The discussion continues as the sunset approaches and the food is consumed. A soft twilight accompanied by a gentle leaf-rustling breeze wafting over the lake finds Mary looking at Michael with a feeling of...pride? Yes, she feels proud that this man (who's come dangerously close to the 'L' word) seems so real in the things that matter. 'Maybe he won't hurt me', she muses. Salvation Mary adds,

"You know, I was raised Baptist. And it's always been a great comfort to me. There was always someplace good to go...Good people, good fellowship, good music..."

"Yeah, that music's what led me to you", Whitey agreeably recollects of their first encounter.

"You old rascal. You are a good man...but you've never been totally comfortable in my church; admit it."

"No, woman. You're right...it's true. I Love you and I respect your beliefs. But...I can't buy the whole program."

"Why not?"

"Well, I just don't feel a connection to the whole thing. Some White dude that lived 2,000 years ago…in the desert…some White God…with a long white beard…that killed *millions* of people. No, I feel best when communing by the seashore…just walking alone with the sky above. That's when I feel God best. Not dressin' up one day a week to hear someone tell me how not to go to hell."

"Whitey, you believe in hell-or heaven?", Michael wonders.

"I believe in an afterlife. I've wondered about heaven and hell… Sometimes I think they both occur on earth. But why, for thousands of years, have people felt that hell is a hot burning place and heaven is a cool oasis with gardens and rivers and streams? I came up with two ideas…course the third is that Baker's got it right, but that's just too much to bear. First idea is that all people of the book-the Jews, Christians and Moslems-all sprang from the desert. Now, what's the worst day to a desert dweller? A day that's hot as hell! What's the best day to a desert dweller? The day they come upon an oasis with gardens and cool water! Too simple? I don't know. How about this one…What if heaven and hell are things we remember from long ago? Like a period in the earth's history when sulphur and volcanoes ruled the atmosphere…and then a gentler time came…and it's all ingrained in us somewhere?"

"I like the desert dweller idea. Makes sense. It also ties into another idea. In the Bible and the Koran, I could never get why pigs were so bad…'forbidden to eat swine flesh.' It's because they're omnivorous. They could literally destroy a marginal culture…in a land with sparse vegetation…a desert. But…every once in a while, I think I'll eliminate pork from my diet. I mean…what if they're right?!"

"Dad, you're a bacon freak…"

"I know. But, I think about it."

"You know Dad, Mom used to take me to church once in a while. I was never comfortable there…at least, not in the services. Met some nice people though…and that made me feel good. I think the more people believe in something good, the gooder they'll be. As a matter of fact, if they'd quit talking about the devil and sin and hell…I guess I'd kind of like going. But, I don't want to hear philosophy. How many churches are there? How many religions? All of them have their own version of how to get to heaven and most of them, that I know about, say you've got to do it *their* way…or you're going to hell. Somebody's wrong! If you ever wonder why my generation doesn't go to church, doesn't watch the news…"

"Just MTV…", Michael daddily squirms in as Skates adds,

"I'm sorry, Mary…I'd watch your show!" This strikes a chord with Whitey, who feels compelled to chime in,

"It's funny, Mary. You're sitting here with, at least, three of us that don't watch much TV and four of us who didn't even know who you were 'til a few days ago. (He starts to crack a wide grin) that must make a TV personality feel pretty bad…except-one of us-is, maybe, fallin' in love with you…" at this Whitey guffaws and has to hold his belly as he gets up out of his chair, so that he can laugh freely.

"Whitey, sit down. (Mary Diana says half-joking and half embarrassed) Now, let Skates finish his thought", she finishes; thus impressing Michael with her attention to his son.

"Like I was saying, my generation is calling your bluff. It's just too confusing trying to figure out whose story is true. So, we're making up our own story."

"And, what is it?" Mary Diana inquires.

"I don't know, yet. I know it involves friends, real friends. And it involves having fun. Let's face it, you grow up…and what?…work?"

"Skates, I actually like my job", MD says.

"Is that something to look forward to? I also want something that involves adrenaline…some risk", he references an earlier thought. "I think that's one reason we like computers and games. If you get really good, it's a world you control."

Michael cuts in, "Son…is Love in there somewhere? You know my generation challenged a lot, too. (and under his breathe, mutters) Maybe that's why your generation is so confused."

"I know, Dad. I've seen pictures of you with long hair and loud shirts. And yeah, love's important…but what is it?"

"Do you believe that I Love you?"

"Yeah, but you weren't there…all the time. I mean I think you're cool, for a dad. My friends think so, too. But I've been surrounded by people that used that word and weren't there…or didn't want *me* there. How do I know what that word means…like you mean it?"

"Well, think of Aunt Sarah…She's always been available to you. She Loves you…truly Loves you…unselfishly. She's taken you on trips… always comes to your birthdays…and Christmas. Does that seem like Love?"

"Yeah, I guess so. But she wasn't always there either."

Mary Diana has a need to jump in here,

"Skates, Love has to be *felt*…inside…to be received from the outside." Michael thinks, 'God, this is starting to seem like an intervention', but, nevertheless, adds,

"I Love you forever. I Love you beyond anything but God. Somewhere inside you, isn't there a spot that *knows*…that can sense…something bigger than you? Something in your heart?"

"Yes, But, it's overpowered by something that scares me…that says, I can't be too soft or I'll get hurt."

"I wish that Love in your heart gave you the confidence to feel it all the time. I feel like I've failed to give you the only true thing there is. You've got to have **Love**", Michael summates.

"You know what I think?", Whitey dryly observes, "He's young. Give him a little time. Skates, what would make you believe in Love?"

Skate jumps on this chance to extract himself from the spotlight. He's been close to tears a couple of times. Now he breaks into a grin and, waiting for the grown-up reactions, says,

"If Jesus came again."

"Ho, ho. Clever, little man", says Mary Diana. She notices that Mary Rose is looking on somewhat disapprovingly. She imagines that she may be perceiving this talk as an attack on her beliefs. So, MD decides to change the subject, not realizing she'll be getting Whitey in hot water over the Marsilius Sandile incident.

"You were speaking of adrenaline a few minutes ago; you guys sure must have had some 'rush' with that character the other night, huh?"

Whitey slides down in his chair; but he's too big for this little lawn chair to hide him. He hasn't told his wife of this incident at all. It would only upset her. And…it does.

"What 'character', Mary?"

"Oh, (She answers, trying to remove her lovely foot) I thought you had heard." Whitey decides to fess up and get it over with,

"Michael found out who robbed him and I helped him give the boy a talking to, that's all."

"Was this the boy that held him up *with a gun*?…after leaving *our* place?"

"Yes."

"And where did this 'talking to' occur?"

"Out back. In the wood shed."

"A man with a gun…out back…in our wood shed? Whitey Grayer, I swear I could smack you…"

"Now, Mary. You know I'd never put either one of us in jeopardy. It just felt like the right thing to do. Michael wanted to try and save this boy…talk some sense into him."

"You should've told me…before it happened."

"Listen. Why don't you all just keep the pie for later. I think I've, uh, got some explaining to do." He's as light and gentle as he can be. He's slightly embarrassed and he knows his wife is as upset with the religion talk as with this untimely revelation. His mate is upset and he doesn't want to spoil the event for the others; so he excuses Mary Rose and himself and they take their leave. Michael, Mary Diana and Skates are left alone in the dusky darkness with the light from the porch softly glowing on their faces. Mary apologizes. She didn't mean to upset Whitey's wife; she was just trying to be considerate by changing the subject. Skates apologizes for getting into religion so much and Michael adds,

"I started it. I just thought that, with a man as open as Whitey, his wife of so many years wouldn't be surprised about that kind of discussion. I'll call him later…make sure they're all right…Mary, does this kind of discussion bother you?" he adds (mostly to impress upon Skates that it's good to check on your progress in any discussion; but *especially* with a female-with potential).

"No. I thought you might have gathered that by now." To which he light-heartedly replies, "I thought so. Just checking (to put her back in control, he says) Hey, boss…when is that roundtable coming up?"

"Before the 'resurrection'. By then, it'll be big news…if Baker's prediction comes true. Listen. I think I'm going to turn in. But thanks. I had a good time." The manner in which this is spoken makes Michael feel she isn't having that good of a time right now. He walks her to her car.

"Mary. What's the matter?"

"Nothing, Michael. I've just got some notes to make…and I know you want to spend some time with your son."

"You sure? I guess you've got a lot on your mind. But something's going on in there."

"I'm just feeling fat…"

"What?", he says in genuine disbelief as he steps back to look at her to see if she grew while he blinked. "You look great!"

"But…what if I was fat?"

"What? Don't you know about beauty? It shines! And so do you."

"No, I don't. That's just a reflection of you." This is spoken in such a way that it doesn't seem like a compliment; more of a warning that she doesn't want perfection assumed of or assigned to her. He doesn't know why she has said this. There are some arguments that can't be won at a particular time even if the two people really like each other. Some *thing will* get confusing. Discretion is the better part of valor; or the coward lives to love again.

"Mary. I Love you (he says off-handedly; but honestly). Not so much as I will…But, I think you should just go home, have a good sleep, take five and call me in the morning. I Love you." He kisses her on the forehead while holding her arms. She's receptive; but leaves in a suddenly sullen mood.

As Michael watches her start driving down the road, he shakes his head and smiles. He walks back around lakeside where his son is still sitting, looking up and contemplating the stars.

"Dad, think we'll ever go to the stars?"

"I think I've been to a couple, pretty vague, though. You know, I think our souls travel the universe…in an unearthly body. I think that's heaven. It sounds scary, being without a body…floating…God knows what happens to time. It probably bends and contorts in all kinds of ways we can't even imagine. But…I suppose you get used to it…You know…earlier…you were talking about 'lonely'. I'm feeling pretty lonely right now, even though you're sitting right there. It's not that I don't Love you…You just don't feel as good as her!…I guess you've just got to be grateful for what you've got, when you've got it. You never know when it's coming or how long it'll be there. Just appreciate it." Skates comes over and gives his Dad a hug. "Dad. I Love you. I'm going to bed." One thing of which Michael's proud is that his son has no trouble showing his affection. Michael couldn't let him be any other way.

Now, Michael's alone. Contemplating the stars and remembering a tune from a record his Dad bought when they lived in south Texas,

'Mary Diana,
If you only knew
just how I feel
about you.

You wouldn't be
so mean to me.'
You'd find a place
in your heart.
Mary Diana,
Mary Diana…'

The noon hour of the following day finds Whitey sitting under the big oak. He lifts his head to see a subdued Michael coming his way. They both put on a show of feigned, strained happiness.

"Whitey, how'd it go? After you left, I mean?"

"I caught a little 'hell' on earth…But, it'll be OK. Just a little time."

"Good. My Mary got a little weird, too. Hopefully, just a little time will solve that, too. You going to see Baker's rally tonight?"

"I don't think so. Mary Rose needs a hand after I get off work. I don't even want to mention this…right now. Baker's not that far off from the kind of preachin' she's used to…Did you realize you just took Baker's name in vain?"

"What!?"

"I mean you're going to see, what has been called, an appearance by Christ…and you described it as 'Baker's rally'. If that's how *you* think of it; what is everyone *else* calling it?"

"I don't know. Stupid, huh? Wanta hear something on a related note? I had a vision of Jesus the other night. I haven't told anyone. It wasn't like a dream; it just 'was'. Call me crazy, whatever; but it happened."

Whitey momentarily stares at his lunch partner thinking, 'Maybe he is crazy.'

"What did he say?" being polite and entertaining the possibility that maybe it is true.

"He said his message was so simple. To Love God and worship God with all your heart. He's tired. He wants to rest…He was funny, too. He had a sense of humour."

"I've always thought there was something missing from the Bible. A sense of humour. That's it. Life doesn't have to be miserable. Much of it can be happy."

"Ain't easy, is it?"

Laughing, Whitey says, "Not all the time, no, it isn't."

"Fuckin' nuts, isn't it?…"

Now that Michael has his stride back; he wants to call his future bride.

"Mary, Michael here. Do you want me to meet you at the cross later today?"

"Yes, can you be there a little after 5?"

"I'll be there as close as I can."

"Michael, I'm…I didn't mean to get strange on you. I'm just trying to work out some things. Listen, Mose is going to shoot the 'roundtable', OK?"

"I understand; he's the pro. I'd like to be there, though…", he says questioningly.

"That's fine. Day by day, OK?"

"Just a little time…"

"What?"

"Mary, I look forward to seeing you."

Straight up at five o'clock, Michael beats it out of the showroom and heads down San Jacinto Avenue. He gets only a few blocks before realizing this path won't get him to his destination very quickly. There are lines of curious cars lined up leading to the cross. Luckily, he's learned a couple of back routes that take him to a small street near the church buildings on the far side of the cross complex. This hidden area of quiet, shaded streets is very beautiful and rarely seen; even by many locals. The bay is just a half block from here with many graceful two and three story homes fronting it. Almost all of these homes have extremely long wooden piers that run out over the marshlands. Most of these piers are about

300 feet long to guarantee access to water at low tide. The variance of the tides is astounding. Waves can lap at your door or be so far out as to require a spyglass to capture water. These streets are narrow and lined with moss-hung oaks that give the area a deep south ante-bellum look. Michael parks as close as he can to the church buildings without violating any property or parking ordinances. As he walks toward the church property; he's glad to notice that, as yet, there are few people assembled. He figures that, most likely, they are up the street at TG's tent show. As he crosses the street and walks briskly toward his rendezvous with Mary Diana; he notices the same white Plymouth he saw the other day…off a bit…in the distance. He swears it appears that Father Leonard is giving Grace a little kiss just before they exit the car. Hey, it's none of his business. He's never understood the prohibition against priestly pro-creation. At least this priest is after a girl! Michael's insight into Jesus (not his vision thereof; but his lifetime of contemplation thereon) has led him to believe that it's quite possible that Jesus and Mary Magdalene had a thing. Would that lessen Jesus' lesson? Not to him. This 'possibility' might even enhance Jesus' message. Michael's interpretation of Jesus is that Jesus was trying to teach Jews to be good Jews. And that in the broader interpretation, he was trying to serve as an example of how we all should live-by honoring God. It is also his belief that Jesus never intended for a religion to be founded in his name. If he did, he thought Jesus fortunate to have died early in his ministry. This prevented him from being the one to screw it up; as just about every religious visionary did that lived for any great length of time. No, it was left to future 'Christians' to screw it up with dogma and human interpretation of divine revelation.

There's the cross. Tall and majestic. There's Mary. Cute and professionally perky. (Just open the tent and see all the people.)

"Hey, Mary", and kisses, 'hello.'

"Ready, big guy? Let's walk over to the tent and see what TG's got in store for today."

Before they proceed very far, Michael is surprised to see Mr. H standing near the vestibule of the church staring up at the cross.

"Mr. H, what are you doing here?"

"Hi, Michael, just contemplating the past, the present and the future." This side of Mr. H is more philosophical and, also, more forlorn than Michael has ever seen. He had never been sure that Mr. H even had a side such as this.

"Mr. H, this is my friend, Mary Diana, from 20-20."

"The TV show?", he says since he had never seen Mary at the dealership.

"Yes, sir. Good to meet you. I'm in town covering this phenomenon regarding Jesus."

"I guess that explains all this camera gear you're carrying…" He looks at both of them and says, "I may want to talk to you…" Then he turns to Michael. "Michael. At work tomorrow…come and see me. Will you?"

"Sure. Yes, sir. I hope you're OK."

"Thanks, yeah, I'm fine", he says wistfully.

Mary and Michael continue walking toward the tent. When they are a respectful distance away from Mr. H; they exchange glances meaning, 'What was that all about?' No time for discussion now though as Michael takes the camera from Mary…to lighten her load in the gentlemanly fashion.

As they reach Baker's area, they see that the crowd at the tent is huge. It spills out into the street and onto the adjacent baseball diamond and even to the jammed parking lot. Not everyone is going to get a great view of this event. It is quite a spectacle. Baker has a racially mixed gospel choir, resplendent in purple robes, belting out soulful vocals to the delight of the crowd. Michael loves gospel music when done right. And this is a great group. He thinks it's truly a shame that their talents are being wasted on promoting this charlatan. At times, Michael has been known to begin mornings by blasting a bagpipe rendition of

'Amazing Grace' on his home stereo. Just as he's thinking this; the choir bursts into that song. Off at the far back fringe of the crowd, Michael notices Leonard…apparently mouthing the words of that beautiful song to Sister Grace. Mary diverts his attention with,

"Michael, maybe we should go get a good spot at the cross. If this entire group marches down there en masse we may have trouble getting a good shot."

"Well, don't you want to shoot this?"

"I guess I can stomach it a little longer…But let's leave before he starts laying on hands, OK?"

As 'Amazing Grace' ends, Baker emerges from the rear of the tent. He's accompanied by his long-time companion, Elisha. The crowd roars it's approval and you can almost taste the Baker's relish of this moment as they acknowledge the adoration of the masses by throwing kisses and waving and smiling. As Baker takes center stage, he launches into one of his cliché-ridden speeches; whipping the multitude into an even wilder frenzy. Now the fever pitch he has been trying to elicit is reached. And with a sweep of his hand he summons the crowd to silence. "Now (his voice booms out over the mike), I'd like a moment of silent prayer…for our brother…Jesse Rod. In just a moment, he's going to come out and tell you the incredible story of how he saw Jesus…and Jesus led him-to me…and this ministry…how we came to be here to witness that magnificent event of which we *all* shall soon reap the GLORY! HALLELU-JAH!" With that, he raises his hand as if reflecting the light of God onto the flock. After a silent moment, he signifies the end of prayer with, "A-MEN. And now, a humble man…make him feel welcome…one touched by God. One of us. God's messenger-Mr. Jesse Rod!" The crowd thunders it's approval as the meek man peeks out from the backstage curtain. Elisha flashes a huge toothy smile accented by garish make-up (that could probably be seen, unaided, from Uranus) and set off by gigantic lashes. She has on a purple outfit and matching purple tinged wig. She advances toward the curtain and offers her hand to Jesse to coax him out of the darkness. Michael has this in focus and leans to Mary, "If I was a shy guy, just the sight of her would make me run for cover." Rod finally emerges and Baker embraces him and hands him the mike,

"Friends, my name is Jesse Rod." The crowd applauds and then, respectfully, quiets so this innocent man may be heard.

"A few weeks ago..I was a lost man", his voice is tremulous but resolute. Again, Michael leans to Mary,

"He's probably the only honest man up there", Rod continues,

"But…at a low point…and with no warning (he raises his hand and points in the direction of the cross; the look on his face is fixed, as if still holding his vision in sight) Jesus' face appeared as clearly as anything I'd seen in twenty years. I didn't know what to do. I just fell down and sobbed. And then…miraculously…I was led to call Reverend Baker. He fed me, clothed me and now…he's brought me here. I don't know what the future will bring. I only know what the past has been. And right now…is the best time. God bless you, Rev. Baker…and Mrs. Baker."

As the throng erupts once more and the Bakers bask in the glory, the meek Rod slips back into anonymity behind the curtain and overhears Tabarnac bellowing into a cell phone in his strange accent (it seems to be a mix of Arabic, French and American English),

"Don't you dare to threaten us! We will bury you! We know who you are; we will expose you-your wife, son and grandson to the whole town if you do not bend to our will. If that fails…we will kill you." Here he pauses for whomever is on the other end of the line. Rod watches as Tabarnac grows, visibly, more and more agitated and finally, spitting out,

"Mr. Harrison, you may be a rich man here-but you are nothing. Do you know where your grandson is right now? No?! Well, I do! Do not threaten us. Do not back out now!" Furiously, Tabarnac slams shut his cellular mouthpiece, he turns and notices Rods startled look and then…rushes towards him.

"What did you hear, pig?!" He grabs the hem of Jesse's garment and forces him to his knees. Jesse is immediately cast into that mental confusion from which he emerged only weeks ago. He is speechless. He can't find any words with which to answer his inquisitor. Tabarnac continues his harangue; but can see that the poor little man has crumbled, "You heard nothing! Remember, nothing!".

"It is as you say." The words fall involuntarily from his mouth and inch along the floor. Tabarnac releases him and Rod slowly slinks out the exit into the back lot of the tented tabernacle amidst the crowing busses and liveried limos. Suddenly he knows that, once again, he has been deceived by the world. The portraits of Baker and the sworded Jesus stare down at him from Baker's big bus. Once again he's a little man crushed under society's weight. He peers around the side of the tent and realizes that he, a messenger of God, will not witness today's revelation. The man who saved him is a traitor to his own message. Even in this clouded state, this man of dubious mental acuity, and on the verge of an almost unsalvageable mental breakdown, realizes that it is Jesus that gave him his moment of bliss. Right now, he must disappear; back into the unseen shadow world where the homeless reside. Right now, he'll retreat to where the trolls hang, under a bridge, near a filth filled creek to fight his demons. For the moment, he will resist a return to inebriation.

"Onward Christian soldiers,
Marching as to war.
With the cross of Jesus
Going on before…"

Baker is in full voice, leading the throng in song, marching to the cross. As the joyous group reaches the cross, Baker plants a mock cross (that has been carried in mock Jesus fashion by three Baker flockers) near the olive trees and begins,

"Brothers and sisters, today we will bear witness to the power of Christ! All of us-here…out of all humanity, **we** will see Jesus! This day has been foretold for two thousand years! And we shall see it!"

The accompanying crowd is enormous. The church grounds are shoulder to shoulder with people. They cover the asphalt of San Jacinto Avenue. They occupy the parking lot of the Best Western and Super 8 across the street. Still more lean from the balconied rooms trying to see the announced wondrous sight. Anticipation grows. Murmurings begin. Mumbled prayers. A sense of dread. A shred of hope. Time is compressed as sundown nears and the moment comes close. Baker calls for silent prayer and asks that all bow their heads, while he keeps one eye peeled. In the portico of the church stand Mary and Michael with camera at the ready.

Even though no rain appears in the heavens, a rainbow appears that is a perfect semi-circle from visible horizon to horizon. The cross is framed underneath the red, blue and yellow display. The cross is cast in the beautiful gold of a softening sun. A form moves across the waters causing ripples to form and sending wavelets to gently lap at the shore. As the essence of the form moves landward, it coalesces into a cloud-like shape. And…as it nears the cross, it passes through the cross and takes shape just in front of the top of the cross. It is now that all can see a holographic image of a Christ-like form. It's three dimensional in the sense that if one were able to move around the image, it could be viewed from all sides. People that have moored their boats behind the cross are even able to see an image. This aspect of the appearance will be learned later as Mary interviews various witnesses. Another thing she will learn is that different people see different images; much like Baker's Jesus vs. Michael's Jesus. Some see a benign and loving face; others a crown of thorns and an anguished expression. As God plans, the image is pho-tographable. The better to disseminate, my dear. The words to follow will be the same to all here and hearing, as they will be the same heard by all those to see and hear media coverage later. For this is only an announcement.

"Hear me, children of God
I appear to you today to tell you

one true thing.
The message of our Creator
will be delivered by me
to you
in seven days.
Tell those whom you Love
and those whom you fear
to take heed.
In seven days. Shabat.
I will be here at noon.
Be not afraid,
God is with us."
With that simple statement, the image vanishes.

Elisha has made her way through the crowd and whispers to TG,

"TG, we may be in trouble with Harrison. Tabarnac says to pass the plate." TG looks shocked. Hadn't Jesus promised him that he'd receive his reward? He hands the mike to her and tells her to solicit; he has been proscribed from doing so. Though, surely, he has done a thousand things against the will of God; he will not disobey a direct order. So, Elisha exhorts the crowd,

"Brothers and sisters, dip deep into your pockets as our friends pass among you. It's been a long and expensive trip for us to be here. We could sure use some love offerings…just to support our ministry in this great endeavour. Hey, didn't my husband tell you that Jesus would be here?! Now give! Give to the glory of God and Thank God Baker!" Baker's minions begin wading through the crowd with wicker baskets to collect additions to Baker's millions. Many chunk huge wads of cash into the baskets. They just *saw Jesus*! God, wouldn't you?

Legumbres Mixta

Quantities vary with need.

Cut 2-3 yellow squash into triangles. Cut +/-8 ozs. white mushrooms in thin slices from top to bottom. Cut a bunch of slender carrots on the diagonal.

Add above ingredients to a cast iron skillet in which one large pat butter has just been melted. Saute' until 'shrooms turn a gray-brown (about 5 minutes over a low flame). Add ¼ cup water (to create steam) and another pat butter and cover. Cook until veggies obtain a nut-like consistency (about 10 minutes).

Eat.

Baker's Relish

(contributed by Wade Lewis)

A good dipping sauce. Can be used for onion rings, fries, veggies, etc. This recipe's quantities are at your whim and taste.

The background and primary taste is orange marmalade. My taste dictates adding one large diced onion. It should be a St. Augustine Sweet or a Vidalia. Then, depending on your capacity for heat, add an appropriate amount of Datil Pepper Mustard Relish. Swirl and consume.

CHAPTER SEVEN

Round Yon Table

Baker has gotten wind of the roundtable discussion which, it has been decided, will take place inside the main sanctuary of Nuestra Senora de la Leche Perpetuo and will precede the next 'appearance'. Some of the participants have expressed reticence about said locale; but, perhaps because of yesterdays appearance, have acquiesced. It has been determined that there will be no audience and that it will be taped; not live. Baker, Mary has decided, will be allowed to participate. She's determined that, though he will distract from the scholarly mood of the show as originally conceived, this may be a way to expose his true nature. She did, however, nix the request to include his wife.

Meanwhile, back at the dealership, Michael remembers that Mr. H. requested to see him. On his desk he sees, after the daily car shuffle, a note addressed to him.

It's a handwritten note from Mr. H.,

Mr. Wade,

Please make arrangements to see me

today at 2 P.M.

Sincerely,

Bentley Harrison, II

The guy may be a tough old businessman, but he does have class, Michael thinks.

Several people at the showroom are deliriously discussing what happened at the church. The front page of the 'Light' has a full color picture of the plainly visible, but grainy, image of Jesus in front of the cross. Most of the people who were actually there fell into, but, a few limited categories. There were Baker's followers, who, though delighted, pretty much took it in stride. They expected it, it was foretold by their 'leader'. They believe the next appearance may well be the rapture. Many of them are currently out telling others (whom they secretly hope will go to hell), 'See, I told you so!'. There were those from the Catholic Church who, today, are busily lighting candles and mouthing the rosary as beads quickly slip from finger to finger. A third, and quite large contingent, was of the curious crowd seekers. This group makes up a considerable portion of the human race. These are 'event' driven people. These are the people who become mobs when properly whipped up. They possess the 'pack' mentality. They populate discos, dance halls, huge rock concerts and so on. This group, being so large and diverse of personality, had the most widely varying reactions. Some were altogether moved by the appearance. They felt relieved, as if this is what they had been roaming from event to event in search of for so long. Others were totally unbelieving. Perhaps they were too used to laser light shows, illusions and special effects. This…was just another show.

The general public did not attend. To most, it was just another gathering of the rabble. But now, as news reports have circled the globe, some people are getting concerned. What should they do? What should they believe? To whom should they turn? Suddenly, these questions took on an import unprecedented in anyone's lifetime. Some cruise the instantaneously created web-sites…like www.jesus.org or www.backslash-backstab.endays.com…ad infinitum, ad nauseum. This isn't like hurricane preparedness. If you anticipate the worst, you realize there *is* no shelter, no evacuation destination. If you anticipate the best; you just get happy. The majority falls into the large middle. They're concerned. And they may make moderate adjustments in lifestyle, just in case. But, really, what would most of us do if we read (and believed) 'Jesus is coming' ? Michael has decided he will pray more often…to the glory of God…can't hurt. He intercoms Mr. H. to tell him he's ready for their meeting. He is told to come ahead.

"Come in, Mr. Wade, come in." Michael is, once again, surprised to see Mrs. H in the room as well,

"Hello…ma'am",

"Have a seat, Michael", she ushers and Mr. H takes over,

"Michael, we've noticed that you're 'friendly' with that newswoman. I've also noticed that you're different from many of my people here. I don't know what you've heard about my family or my history; but I'm sure you've heard something…"

Michael doesn't want to acknowledge that he has heard a few rumours related to the 'coke' incident and vague mob ties; but he is glad to hear today's discussion won't be about his job, "Go on, sir."

"Diplomatic, aren't you…Michael, we've decided to trust you with some information. Information that's painful to reveal. Maybe it shouldn't be, but pride gets in the way. I want your word…as a gentleman-and I believe you are one, that you will use this information *only* to expose that snake, The Reverend T.G. Baker…and not…to hurt my family."

"I believe I can do that, sir…ma'am. I appreciate the trust…But first, tell me…are you sure you want to do this?"

"I've got to tell somebody and I know that girl of yours wants to nail Baker."

"Well, go ahead."

"That day Baker came in and met with us; remember?"

'Yes, sir."

"His 'henchman', that Tabarnac, had given him a whole file on us; full of everything I've tried to bury since I left Georgia. I could have gone into the family business back home; but I didn't want to follow my father's path."

"What business was that?"

"Like I said….'Family' business, the 'Family'…" Mr. H sees the confused wrinkle in Michael's brow and adds, "The mob, the Georgia mafia. I wanted out. My dad made me a one-time offer. He gave me some money and told me I could never come home. I came down here, bought this dealership and skated along pretty good for a long time. Then, my son got the bright idea of taking some drugs up north. He was so high by the time he got to D.C. that he got busted just for lookin' nervous. I had nothing to do with it; although I did manage to get the charges dropped. But…if Baker strung these two unrelated things together…it could ruin me in this town."

"People are more forgiving and more forgetful than you may realize…"

"It could hurt my wife and family."

"What do you want me to do?"

"I'm not sure…it's tricky. He used this information to force me to give him one million dollars worth of land I own outside of town…"

"W.I.C.C.A…", Michael mutters.

"What?"

"W.I.C.C.A., the Christian theme park Baker talked about; he's blackmailing you."

"Yeah, well that's not the worst part. Yesterday, I told Tabarnac I was backing out. He made physical threats…against me and my family."

"Maybe this is a good time for a vacation…"

"I've already told JR to take his wife and our grandson away tonight. And there's one other thing I haven't told you. There is a 'recessive' gene in our family. I've been very unfair to my son…more so to his wife. Did you ever notice this picture?" Mr. H picks up the framed photo of the dark skinned boy on his desk.

"All these years…I had never even told my wife…until last night. In the south, some things are far worse than a checkered past."

"Like what?"

"A checkered family tree…", Mrs. H drops to a still confused Michael.

"What she means is that I've allowed my son to wonder, all these years, if his son is really *his* son…Because I didn't want to tell anyone that, not too far back, on my family tree is a Negro. I've tried to give my grandson everything to make up for the sin of omission I committed on my family. God, I thought I was so strong. I thought I was so smart…" The tough old man turns his face to conceal tears welling up in his eyes. Michael never thought he'd see this. Mr. H composes himself enough to add,

"Yesterday, Tabarnac threatened to kidnap my grandson…and to tell him my secret. It can come from no one but me."

"Why don't you go to the police? You must have friends there…"

"I'd still like to keep most of this quiet. I'd still like to maintain the reputation I have here; even if it is, ultimately, irrelevant. I thought knowing these facts might help your friend know she's on the right track. These people are scum. I'm a hard businessman and I've made a lot of money; but I've never killed anyone or even come close. What do you say, Mr. Wade? Can you help?"

"Let me talk to Mary Diana; see what she says, OK?"

"Thank you."

"Yes. Thank you." Mrs. H says with a modest hug.

"Sir, it's not my place…but, maybe, you should try for some family forgiveness."

Michael is granted the rest of the day off to go huddle with Mary Diana at the hotel. As he pulls up to a parking spot on the street, he's wondering if this woman is going to follow through on her feelings for him or leave him in the dust of this small town. As he makes his way through the lobby and up the elevator to her door, he puts his thoughts aside and knocks. Mary hurriedly opens it,

"Come in, I'm on the phone with Lordstown."

He enters as she hustles back to the phone and his arms feel empty. He really wanted to give her a big presumptuous hug.

"OK, yeah, I've got that. But no other proof was ever found? Uh-huh. OK. Thanks. You've been a big help." As Mary hangs up the phone, she rushes over to Michael and gives him the squeeze for which he's been aching. He responds by enfolding her in his eager arms.

"Michael, I didn't mean to push you out of my heart. I was just afraid to let you in. But I'd like to try. No guarantees. You're here and I'm all over the place. But let's try, OK?"

"You don't have to talk me into it. I'm willing. So, what was that on the phone?"

She drags him over to the bed and says,

"That can wait a bit. Think you can do again what you did before?"

"I bet I can."

"You know Michael, the way you are with your son, other people, with me…It makes me feel I can talk to you about almost anything."

Then she pulls him to her and kisses him. This time will be longer, slower and deeper.

Later, after they emerge from under the covers both rested and energized, they slip into the plush robes the hotel provides and begin to discuss the day's findings.

'Mary, I've got to tell you what Mr. H told me. But he doesn't want it used publicly."

Michael recounts the tale anyway; so that she'll be up to speed. When he's finished, Mary has a deep, pondering countenance,

"This is interesting. I've been doing some long distance sleuthing in Baker's hometown. It led me to a union official there who told me that a few years ago something similar happened in Lordstown. A guy named Jimmy Hofheinz was the local union treasurer. Baker got some dirt on the union and this guy Hofheinz. Eventually, Hofheniz disappeared. But what came out is that, afterwards, Baker owned a big chunk of union property. That property had been part of the union pension fund. Baker's headquarters Tabernacle now sits on that land. No one could ever prove anything because all the paperwork was in order and the only guy that knew the truth was missing."

"Wow. So, I guess these hairy vicious christians are more dangerous than we ever knew. The Harrisons *are* in danger. You ever had a death dream…or vision?"

"What! What do you mean?"

"Many years ago, in Mexico, I was at a place called Coatzacoalcos. One night I was in my room and I saw a vision; like a pale ghostly skeleton. The feeling transmitted to me was that someone was going to die. It didn't scare me. It was more like a warning. The next day a hurricane blew in and three fisherman I knew died just as their boat entered the harbor. The boat caught a big wave and slammed down hard on the surface of the water and just exploded. The first time I saw Tabarnac; I had almost the exact same feeling."

"You know what he looks like to me?"

"No, what?"

"Like a combination of a gaunt Omar Shariff and Dracula."

"Ha,ha-that's pretty accurate."

"If Harrison doesn't want me to use this info; what good is it?"

"I wish there was a way to hear what goes on when those three are alone..."

"Maybe there is, maybe there is."

The day of the 'roundtable' arrives and all are meeting at the church. Father Leonard has suggested a seating arrangement where all participants may easily view one another. In front of the altar, he has placed the chairs in a semi-circle. Mary Diana will be in front of them facing the altar. She's decided to use two cameras at angles to one another as to get a sweep of the semi-circle. Moses will man one camera and an associate of his will operate the other. The panel members have been asked to utter any prayers they wish to offer in private, prior to the meeting.

Outside, the town has begun to swell to bursting with media types. And, while MD's discussion will air on only one network, plans have been made by all major carriers to cut away to San Jac at the time of Jesus' announced appearance. There are even plans for international feeds. Most major sporting events have decided to use their giant screens to televise the event and thus avoid any potential customer drain. Judgment day on the big screen.

Elsewhere in town, Jesse Rod has been hiding out under his favorite old bridge down near the San Jacinto Winery where he used to do late night dumpster dives to drain the dregs from discards. He is resisting the temptation to return to his old ways of getting high; but–he can no longer remain silent. He's about to erupt with conflict; though his vision remains true in his head. He is filled with anger towards those that betrayed him and mocked his vision. What can he do? He's just a bum. At this precise moment, a careless pedestrian passes over the foot-bridge above Jesse and, with no thought of re-cycling, wads up his newspaper and tosses it over the side. It lands right next to Jesse. As he picks it up and smooths the edges, he notices the story of the religious discussion taping at sundown today. He looks skyward and decides, for better or worse, he will try to crash the taping and expose Baker on national TV. He doesn't know taping from live. He only knows he must act. He climbs the short, grassy bank up to street level and begins strid-ing towards the cross. As he emerges into the light, a glint of sun reflects off a nearby steeple and momentarily blinds him. For the next few moments, everywhere he looks, he sees the sign of the cross suspended in his field of vision.

The studio/church has no audience; save for Leonard, Grace and Michael. Mary wants control of the questions. There will be no public Q&A here. The communicants are seated and ready. On the left is Tenzin Gyatso. Next to him is Rabbi Neil Tzedakah. Then there's Father Ben Asher; the ordinary of this diocese. Next to him is Yusef ibn Hisham. And, finally, on the far right is the Reverend TG Baker. Mary opens the session thus,

"Good evening. Thank you all for agreeing to be here. Let's start with one of the oldest religions first. Mr. Gyatso, what is the Buddhist impression of the recent appearance and announced return of Jesus?"

Mr. Gyatso is older in person than his phone voice indicated. He's a gentle appearing man in saffron robes and short clipped hair (that seems to be graying) and simple, circular spectacles.

"I would say…that it is difficult to deny a messenger from God. It would also appear that, if this is Jesus and he does return, this could go towards proving what we have, all along, said regarding re-incarnation."

"Thank you. Now, Rabbi, what would you say?"

"First, let me say, what a pleasure it is to be here...with my contemporaries to discuss this momentous event." The middle-aged Rabbi is in a dark gray business suit set off by a black yarmulkah. He's a bit scholarly looking...earnest, robust, with a trim goatee. His voice would remind some of the old vaudevillian, Georgie Jessel.

"I would say 'Is this the 'man', Jesus?' or 'Is this the messiah?' Remember, please, to us, there is a difference. Jesus was a Rabbi; same as me...Greater? Perhaps...More famous? For sure. The Jewish people have expected a messiah for centuries. But, now, when it happens...no longer will it be for the Jewish people only; it will be for the whole world. There is too much suffering...everywhere. The world must be healed. As humans, we have the ability to heal one person at a time. Perhaps, if this is the messiah, he could help us. He could help us heal more of us, more quickly. Let us hope it is true; let us not lose faith if it is not."

"Thank you, Rabbi. That was a very thoughtful answer. Faith and truth. Father Asher, how do you see this phenomenon?" Father Asher has a sternly curled brow topped by well-trimmed thinning gray hair. His form is also trimly accented by squared shoulders. He appears to be about fifty-five. He could be an American Sean Connery.

"The fact that this is happening on hallowed ground...on Catholic property is significant. It means that we have been right all along. 'Catholic' simply means 'universal'. All people should see the significance of this appearance as an invitation, if you will, to join the Church now and avoid eternal...an eternal, irreversible error."

"Would you call it a miracle?"

"The Church has not declared a miracle. My presence indicates the first step in determining the possibility of a miracle. I would echo my Buddhist brother and say 'it is difficult to deny a messenger from God.' I would also echo Rabbi Tzedakah and say 'this time, it is for the whole world.!'"

"Father, (Mary leans forward for emphasis) on a personal level, is it miraculous?...to you?"

"I have seen nothing, as yet. But...our own Father Leonard has witnessed an appearance of Our Lord. I pray to be granted the same privilege."

"Next we have Yusef ibn Hisham. Mr. Hisham, you're a member of the local Muslim community?"

"Yes, Miss Diana. That is true."

"What is your view of the recent local occurrences?"

"And peace be unto you. I would, also, say that it is difficult to deny a messenger from God. And we, as all religions here, recognize Jesus in some way. We even believe he will come again. Perhaps, it is now. That is wonderful, that is not the point. The final messenger for the whole world has already come. His name is Muhammad, bless his holy name. He is the prophet and messenger of Allah, the most gracious; the most merciful."

Mary has been, purposely, avoiding getting to fidgeting Baker. She thinks it must be killing him to share the stage. Apparently, she's right as Baker suddenly bursts forth,

"You know, the way I see it (he begins to rise from his chair but thinks better of it and leans further into the camera) this happened in the sky! And that's my domain!"

Reflexively, Mary shoots back,

"Either you or the F.A.A.! What about the fact that this happened at the site of an ancient Native American village? Could it be that their ancient, anguished murdered spirits crying out attracted this event?" Mary has gone from moderator/interviewer to editorializing participant in one swell foop.

"Well, little lady (this really pisses off Mary), I don't know about the Indians..."

"No wonder…They're all dead! (Mary decides to switch gears and back up) Look, Reverend…can I just call you TG? 'Reverend' is just too much."

"Yes, yes. TG is fine…" Mary, having resigned herself to the inevitable, asks,

"What is your take on these events?"

Rather than listen to Baker's drivel; let's catch up with Jesse Rod. At this very moment, Jesse has an apocalyptic vision. He decides to confront Tabarnac. He deviates slightly from his path and goes to the tent site; the functioning headquarters of Baker's San Jacinto operation. There seems to be no one at the tent itself; but he notices activity in the main bus. He knocks on the door. Tabarnac opens it; holding a huge wad of cash. Mrs. Baker is close behind and peers around Tabarnac. She too, holds a wad. Jesse summons all of his dormant courage to speak,

"Mr. Tabarnac, I'm marching right over to the church and I'm going to expose you and your boss. You're evil, deceptive snakes and someone's got to stop you." With that, Jesse hightails it away from the bus entrance. He hears Elisha stammer, "Tabarnac, you've got to stop him. Go get him!", as a squall begins to blow in from the bay and turns the air a dark electric gray and fills the air with the smell of water. Tabarnac stuffs the cash into the pockets of his great coat and looks out at the sudden storm with the look of a killer dog unleashed.

"Stupid fool. I warned him!", he spits out to no one and takes his first long stride to undertake the hunt. He sees Rod's shadow flicker by the front edge of the tent complex and purposefully fixes his gaze in that direction. Now, he has the scent. Jesse has to make it down and across the street, in the now driving storm, to get to the sanctuary of the church. His heart is pounding now. He knows he may become a martyr. The pain will be brief; the glory forever; the truth revealed. With each step of Rod's, Tabarnac gains. Jesse keeps looking over his shoulder to see his fate approach and each time he looks he loses a step; thus sealing his fate. Tabarnac is closing in just as Jesse reaches the outer door of the church; Jesse can see a picture of Jesus and Mary inside the glass doors. The picture is flanked by flowers and hangs above a three foot heavy brass cross resting on a simple wooden table. He tugs on the outer door as he feels Tabarnac reach for him. He gets in that door; but before he can reach the inner door–he feels his world go black. Tabarnac is standing over him holding the heavy brass cross. He's holding it as if it's a dull-weighted sword. A flash of lightning causes Tabarnac to feel suddenly seen. With the cross lifted high, he smashes the single, simple light overhead and then continues his deadly arc. Bringing down the cross and burying it in the skull of Jesse Rod. The man who saw the light just in time. Tabarnac bolts out the door.

Inside the debate continues unabated. The storm has dulled outside noises so that they are heard, merely, as acts of God. Rod did not cry out; he simply crumpled and died. Mary asks Yusef ibn Hisham,

"What is the highest attribute of Islam?"

"It is as the name means, submission to God's will, devotion."

"Yes, but how can you expect to be saved when you don't accept Christ; the messenger of God?", asks Father Asher.

"A common misconception. We *do* acknowledge Jesus as the messenger who preceded God's final messenger, Muhammad."

"Do you not see that God has many messengers?", Tenzin adds rhetorically; for to him this is obvious.

"God has had many messengers; but only Islam has preserved, unchanged, the Word of God."

Rabbi Tzedakah is compelled to offer, "Do you not know that the Torah is also painstakingly kept accurate to preserve the exact letter by letter sequence that God dictated to Moses?"

Asher adds, "We believe that our Holy Bible is the inspired word of God and it definitely precedes the Koran." Asher is starting to irritate Hisham and Hisham regales him with tales of the many conclaves that altered and abridged the bible over the centuries as well as the extensive and on-going revisions that continue to alter the words of the bible.

"Christianity and Judaism are a violent and pagan religion; yet we realize our roots as worshipping the same God. God revealed to Prophet Muhammad the true and unsullied Word of God precisely because His Word had become so distorted throughout the centuries that a true and accurate recitation was necessary. The early church popes burned pagan and Gnostic papers by the bushel. The crusaders burned all the books they could find; even ancient Hebrew texts. Cardinal Ximenes burned, in Granada, 80,000 Arabic texts. Calcus witnessed the church altering its own texts to insert the words that leaders of the time wished the people to hear."

Baker feels somewhat intimidated by the scholars surrounding him; but thinks he can score a few points by adding,

"The muslim hordes spread their vile faith by the sword; killing thousands in their path…"

"Muhammad, only reluctantly, took up the sword to avoid persecution. He was merciful to all who accepted the Word of God."

Tenzin tries to steer the talk away from dissent by referring back to a question Mary had posed to Hisham,

"Miss Diana, do you know the highest attribute of Buddhism? It is respect for all living things; the unity of all."

"Thank you, Mr. Gyatso. It's important to remember that we are here (by this, she means the here and now) to discuss an event, not to vent the centuries of hatred and mis-understanding that plague the world. And if it takes the words of Gautama Buddha to remind us; so be it."

Baker bellows belittlingly,

"Oh, Guitama Spitama. You're all pagans and you're going to hell!"

The other members of the panel are shocked by this display of total dis-respect for the thousands of years of shared history. Even the Catholic Church, of late, has reached out to, even, Buddhists. But Mary is ready and asks,

"Do you think lying, cheating, blackmail and murder are things that can send a person to hell?"

"Well, good God, yes!"

"I have here a tape that was made in your bus; would you like to hear it?"

"Well, what is it; some of our gospel singers?"

"No. It's you, your 'wife' and your ass(acid dripping from her tongue)istant, Tabarnac discussing the disappearance of a union official in Lordstown and his burial under the cross at your church and your bribing of a local man here to extract land from him in exchange for your silence about his past..."

Suddenly, a scream pierces the room.

"Moses, hold the tape!", shouts Mary as she rushes to the source of the screams, to her rear, near the entrance to the church. As she opens the door to the vestibule, she sees Grace bending over Jesse Rod. A large pool of blood has spread out and encircled his head, creating a red halo effect on the marbled floor. Grace's hands frame the head; but she can't actually touch it and isn't sure that she should. She can only breathe deeply, quickly. Knowing that she cannot help this poor man. Leonard comes running up and his first inclination is to give this man the last rites; but...is he Catholic? Baker pushes his way forward and exclaims,

"Oh, my God! What happened?"

Mary says, bitterly,

"If you weren't sitting in that room, I'd say you had something to do with it."

Baker rears back to slap Mary and then withdraws as Moses' camera lights flick on to record the death of the messenger, Jesse Rod. Michael goes to phone the police as learned men huddle over the dear departed.

"Who was he?", asks Tenzin.

"He was the man that saw Jesus in the sky", says Mary, reverently. Then she ponders,

"I wonder what he was doing here?"

"He was probably coming to tell me something. I'll bet", Baker says pompously.

"Why is it always about you, Baker?", says Mary, fairly quaking with repugnance.

The police and ambulance lights flicker off the wetted walls of the church as the non-witnesses gather in the post-storm calm and huddle in small groups as they are interviewed by various officers of the San Jacinto P.D.. The body is gurneyed off toward the ambulance for it's trip to the morgue as there is no life left in the body of Jesse Rod. Slowly, the police leave the scene and those remaining congregate in groups of two and three to commiserate. Father Asher is heard asking Rabbi Tzedakah, "Would you consider speaking to one of our youth groups in the near future? I'd like them to know more of 'from whence we came.'"

"It would be my honor, Father." Tenzin is in earshot and Asher asks him,

"Mr. Gyatso, how about you? Would you care to give us some of your knowledge?" "Yes, I would."

So it seems that true hostility has caused to cease the petty hostility that was developing in the earlier dialogue; at least for men of good-will…

"Now listen, young lady (Baker is saying in hushed, but firm, tones as he wags his finger in Mary's face), you better not release those tapes–there are laws against wire-tapping…"

"If you don't get that finger out of my face, I'm going to break it off!"

They both turn to see the source of sudden laughter. It's Michael walking toward them. He's overheard Mary's command and it cracks him up. He addresses Baker through his laughter,

"So, Baker-which came first? The chicken or the chicken-shit? There's no wire-tapping here. Just shut up and go back to your sleazy group of wicked vine-dressers (quoting a bible passage that has always tickled him) and don't (here his voice lowers and his lips curl up around his gums, baring his teeth), don't ever threaten this woman again."

Bakers feels suddenly alone and, uncharacteristically, turns, without a word, and retreats towards his tent site…to find a bug?

"Guess he feels 'bugged'. Did you really do that?", Michael chortles.

Michael and Mary begin to leave the area. Michael puts his arm around Mary's waist. He does this naturally, for the first time, as if it belongs there. He glances back to hear Leonard say to Grace,

"We'd better go change the bulbs in the vestibule."

Sauteed Escarole
and Left-over Chicken

❀

In a large frying pan, put layer of grapeseed oil, garlic (lots-fresh or powdered), ground pepper and salt. Heat 'til hot, then add mass quantities of escarole (which will boil down to a mere shadow of their former selves). Shortly before the greens are done, add thinly sliced left-over cold broiled skinless chicken. At the same time, add thin sliced ginger and sprinkle with sesame seeds. Dribble tamari over mixture. Done when wilted!

Eggplant Maria Diana

Cover bottom of med./large cast iron pot or pan with garlic olive oil (Boyajian has a good one).

Chop 2-3 garlic cloves, several slices of ginger and a handful of chives.

Chop 4 small Spanish onions.

Slice 2-3 long slender flavorful eggplants into ¼ inch thick rounds.

Heat oil. When it sizzles to a few drops of water add:

Garlic first. Then add ginger and chives. Finally, add onions.

Cook and stir 'til onions are shiny and almost opaque.

Add eggplant. Stir and mix.

Add 1 lb. plum tomatoes cut in chunks. Stir and mix to coat.

Lower heat to low and add 3 tbs. chopped dried parsley. Stir and mix.

Add 2 tbs. capers with their liquid. Stir and mix.

Add juice of one Moroccan clementine or other orange/tangerine. Stir and mix.

Continue to cook for several minutes while occasionally stirring.

When eggplant is tender but not mushy-it's ready. Use cook's prerogative and taste it.

When the texture is right for you, remove from heat.

Sprinkle each serving with white pepper and parmesan.

    This dish has a delicate sweet flavor-a culinary coup d'etat.

CHAPTER EIGHT

It's Showtime!

The days of the week are slipping by. And now, as the appointed hour approaches, the town takes on a full-blown circus atmosphere. Valerie sol. Wolfe and her 'Humping for God' troupe have taken center stage downtown. She is the leader of the Sanctified Church of the Ultimate Manifestation. She has many followers holed up at their compound in Montana where they are pretty much self-sufficient and harmless. She seems to be sincere in her belief that we are surrounded by those who have passed on and risen to spiritual heights sufficient to be called Attendants to Vishnu or ATV's for short. One of her teachings is that color is crucial. Purple being the highest color upon which to meditate. This has caused some to call her religion, 'The 7th Ray Adventists'. She is currently traversing the country, in a large mobile home caravan, to awaken people to the coming disaster if we fail to pray hard enough to ward it off. She seems oblivious as to why people snicker at the acronym of her church emblazoned on her vehicles rolling through America. She is an odd mix of spirituality and a female superior attitude due to the fact that men are 'incomplete' as they have no X chromosomes. She had attempted to get Mary Diana to allow her to participate in the 'round-table' but was re-buffed as too non-mainstream. She declared to Mary that she had been told by one of her spirit guides that she would participate. This prompted Mary to off-hand to Michael, "Beware of Wolfes in prophets clothing." As the S.C.U.M. vehicles park around the town square, one might wonder, 'Does 'scum' have a plural?' A further look around town would indicate a resounding-Yes!

A klan style organization known as the Sons of the Beatitudes is parading in white satin robes and hoods. They parade with fiery burning crosses held aloft. Last year, in a nearby town, a shootout had taken place between the SOB's and a Black group protesting their presence.

This confrontation had caused Senator Mims to comment, 'the far White and the far Black agree on one thing, everybody should have guns.' The NRA immediately 'borrowed' this phrase for their own literature. Meanwhile, the Fire Chief in San Jac is trying to get the SOB's to extinguish their crosses for the 'coming' event.

As Michael and Mary were passing through the square and gawking at the wares being hawked; they were suddenly confronted by a young Hare Krishna adherent. "How can you love this woman? She is but flesh and bone and blood and snot…" "But I do Love her, every snot and tittle!" The Hare Hare moved on and passed a group of Virgin puppeteers known as 'The Marion-ettes'. As Michael and Mary move through the crowd, they notice that everyone seems to have a JC Cola. There's a concession over there selling sunglasses endorsed by the Pope (he doesn't really want you to be blinded by the light). Of course, Baker's folks are out there selling Bible Gum and a religious coloring book that explains to young children that the earth is only 6,000 years old and purports to prove it with a mix of science and biblical reference. There are the familiar woven bracelets with the logo WWJD. A well-meaning effort, no doubt; but open to wide speculation. Michael sees one that says WWGD and is told it stands for What Would God Do. He imagines What Would Ghandi Do and Mary retorts with, 'What would Godot Do?'. Many offerings are no doubt sincere; but suspect. One such is the coin minted in Italy, with some pope's blessing, depicting the face of Jesus as interpreted from the shroud of Turin. A nun, of some order, had a vision that Christ said he wanted people to, more often, venerate his face and so she had this coin drawn up. Wasn't there something about 'graven images'?

What is it that attracts us to this sort of thing? For many of the merchants, the answer is profit. For some buyers, it's a desire to express their faith. But for what reason? To ensure a place in heaven? To bring us closer to a chance to be in heaven? To make us feel connected to One who will decide our eventual fate? For good luck? To impress someone? A thousand reasons; a thousand relics.

The murder and the miracle have caused Mary Diana's interview to be pushed up to primetime news in a condensed form. Moses camera work and Mary's reporting have been used by CNN and all the early morning news shows and serve as a great teaser for her 20/20 segment that will air tonight. But she's got to get a little more on tape for some live spots the network is requesting and decides upon interviews with a few 'man on the street' types. She decides that one of these will be Michael. In him, she thinks she may have found a truly sincere man. He has told her that his attitude in life can be summed up by paraphrasing Bertrand Russell. To wit, 'I have three passions that have governed my life:

The longing for Love

The search for knowledge; especially God

and-the almost unbearable pity for the suffering of humankind and how to relieve their pain.'

He has told her of his search for an earthly companion which, though he hasn't directly told her, he thinks to be her. He has read several translations of the Bible, the most illuminating being the Lamsa translation directly from the Aramaic into English. He's read two translations of the Qur'an, the best being that of Arafat El-Ashi (although he's been assured that only Arabic truly communicates the whole of the message). He has read many of the Upanishads, the Book of Tao and a hundred other texts *all* in search of the truth. He has also told her that his ¼ Cherokee blood has led him to seek out unwritten beliefs of Native Americans and other indigenous people wherever he has traveled. And yet, he has asserted, the greatest revelations of pondering the imponderable have always been found inside. In situation after situation he has been granted life and insight in ways that he terms 'the miracles of everyday life'. These are little 'magic moments' from whatever powers run the universe that occur whenever one wonders what course of action should be taken. They guide one to a solution as long as self-ish motives are withdrawn from the question. He believes that ethical choices, both personal and historical, can be reduced to simple things. For instance—'Do unto others as you would have them do unto you'—Jesus. Or, like Dr. Laura—'now, let's turn this around; how would you feel if the same were done to you?' Or, no matter how many times you throw the I Ching, the answer comes down to this— 'What would the honorable man do?' Mary Diana thinks she just might be able to Love this guy. And, as she's planning this 'debut' for Michael, she is creating one of God's magic moments.

"This is Michael Wade, a local man formerly of Miami. Mr. Wade, what's your take on the events in San Jacinto?"

"I believe that all religions spring from a spark of truth, a truth for a particular time or for all time-but none are exclusive from, or superior to, the others. *All* get bogged down and altered by men over the course of time in rhetoric, ritual and dogma. After a while, their objective seems to shift from doing right by God to killing the enemy. *Who* is the enemy? Anyone who disagrees on how to worship God. Look at the Catholics and Protestants, Christians and Muslims, Hindus and Buddhists, Sunni and Shiite; ad infinitum. We have all been created. If you acknowledge that; then you must acknowledge a Creator. We are all products of the Creator; then, are we not all equal before the Creator? Is one of us to be higher than the next? I don't think so. Respect for life and our fellow humans must come first on earth. We cannot raise up ourselves unless one of two things occurs. One, we elevate someone with us. Or, two, we lower someone below us. Of these two, which is the honorable path?" Michael's words seem to be from somewhere beyond him. Sincere; but, almost, otherworldly.

"I say all this to say that Jesus is going to reveal that he wants for us what our Creator wants for us. That is to honor God and recognize that everyday is a miracle. It is up to us to help ourselves by helping others. Do not draw on false mysticism by worshipping idols. This is, plainly and specifically, prohibited in the Ten Commandments. Look at those 10 and add the 'Golden Rule'. You really need little else to lead a good and honest life."

"Is there any particular religion to which you belong?"

"No. I've tried. Lord, I've tried. I was raised Methodist. At an early age, I Loved that feeling of people caring. But, as I grew, I found just as much hypocrisy there as anywhere. No evil intent or anything so blatantly horrible; but dogma and form that are irrelevant to my God. By *my* God, I mean *God*. If God is God; then God *is* that God is—no matter what we try to make of it. I've been to Quaker services, Mormon, Baptist, Catholic, Episcopal, Jewish, holy roller. You name it. If they'd let me in—I'd go.

One thing that bothers me, though…is this…If, on the day Jesus reappears, he says things that cause the religions of the world to change overnight; where will the people of the world go to worship? It's been proven that people who attend church live longer, happier lives…with far fewer divorces. People need the closeness of friends that they feel care for them; that make them feel they matter. For many, religious services meet this need. But, if history holds true (and it usually does), I have little to worry about. They will change little or not at all. They are…too fully entrenched in themselves…and in their ways. Muhammad said that when Jesus returns, he would remain for forty years. If that happens, he will wander the earth…teaching. He's probably fortunate, that in his earlier life, he died just three years after beginning his ministry."

"Why do you say that?"

"In the histories of many religions; those who lived too long often corrupted their own religions by, eventually, contradicting themselves and amending what they earlier had said was the word of God. Now, *was* it the Word of God? Or, were they deluded all along? God is; that God is."

"Is there one religion you think is…a bit more 'correct' than others?" Mary questions; playing devil's advocate.

"In theory…perhaps Jefferson's church-the Unitarians. But, they're so boring. They may be the most humane church, however."

Mary laughs at this and asks (smiling),

"Do you think God has a sense of humor?"

"Oh, I think so. Or, at least, God wishes *us* to have a sense of humor. Whenever we wake up and become aware…don't you think it's *amazing* how often it relates to our realizing that a…particular fear that we had…was totally without foundation? Whenever that happens to me, it makes me laugh…We have so little to fear. Most of us fear death in some way…me; I fear torture-death is easy." Michael is smiling at this as he continues on a different note,

"In one of the dead sea scrolls, the Gospel of Thomas (which contradicts Matthew; Mark, Luke and John *and* Peter), it says that one who **understands** the Words of Jesus will be 'saved'. Just to *understand*–to stand under; as to humble oneself before God, at the feet of the Master, if you will. You needn't believe nor convert. Do you ever wonder why the documents found at Nag Hammadi, after fifty years, still aren't completely available to the public?…Same reason they sealed the Warren Commission report. They are afraid of shaking up the status quo because they have no faith in the ability of their fellow humans to be able to discern the truth on their own. 'We', the general public, are not trusted by our leaders; be they political, religious, financial or otherwise. But, who are they, who have set themselves up as our 'protectors'? They are we; no better-no worse."

"How do you think it all started…this religious morass?"

"I don't know. I don't pretend to know…though, I continue to inquire. At this time in our history, I am more concerned with how it will all end…Do you know where the word 'religion' comes from?"

"No. Where?"

"From the ancient animist beliefs of our forebears. The ancient root of the word 'religion' is 'tree'…from when we worshiped the things around us. Would that we paid the natural gifts of the earth a bit more reverence right now. They are fast disappearing…and they are our sustenance. Even mushrooms were worshipped because of their rapid growth after rain…and the shapes they took on. Some of their properties even offered a perceived way into heaven. I could go on and on…but, let me say this…True religion, though I prefer the word 'spirituality', is not merely mouthing the words of a particular creed; but…living….to the highest precepts of that creed-everyday…by worshipping the many manifestations of God and by not judging the way others worship God. Reach out…to find a common ground among people of goodwill."

"Thank you, Mr. Wade. You'd think Jesus might have appeared to you…"

"Well. He did", Michael says, almost sheepishly-yet still believing there's no harm in revealing this now. Mary's body rolls at this revelation. Mouth agape, she steps back (thinking, 'Jerk. When were you going to tell me this!') and asks,

"And what did he say?"

"Well…basically, that he…(Michael stops mid-sentence and decides to only tell the parts that relate to him)…wants me to be there…at his appearance…and to be a witness…to help him spread his message."

"How will you do that?"

"Right now…I haven't got a clue…But I betcha I do after Saturday!"

"This 'man on the street' is the only one I…uh-we need. Back to you." And she concludes the interview by throwing it back to the network.

"Michael, when were you going to tell me about Jesus?"

"I wasn't sure I was supposed to. But all of a sudden-it seemed right."

"Jesus, Michael, you really threw me."

"Well, Jesus threw me, too."

Time is compressing, spiraling…toward this, potentially, epoch-making event. Accelerated events are occurring…the murder of Jesse Rod, the coming of the second coming. Mary's show starting out as a philosophical discussion, ending up (originally) with accusations at Baker being interrupted by the discovery of a cross buried in a skull in the vestibule. And now a grafted pre-quel of Michael's soliloquy… Things are in a frenzy. Calls begin coming into the network about Michael's appearance in Mary's primetime report. Many of the calls, of course, are for his death. Some see him as a blasphemer of…almost…all religions. But many callers want to know more about him. Many heard the truth in his message. Hugh Downs calls Mary to apprise her of the response. (He still keeps his hand in while he pursues the 'net.)

"Mary, hi, this is Hugh."

"Hugh. What did you think?"

"Crazy situation, eh? Who was that guy? Michael Wade. Did you just pick him out on the street…do you know him?"

"Yes. I do know him. We've gone on a couple of dates since I've been here. I really like him. To tell you the truth (what else would you tell?), I think I may Love him."

"He's really an interesting fellow. We've been getting a large number of calls about him. What do you think he'd say to the idea of a weekly show on, oh…say the nature of God or spirituality…something like that?"

"Hugh, I have no idea what he'd think. Why? Who would produce it?"

"I might; if you'd co-anchor…"

"Really? Interesting. Really interesting. (This excites her.) Hugh, this could be the answer to something I've been thinking about…and, (almost as an aside) several things I've been thinking about. Hugh…Let me talk to Michael and get back to you. OK?"

"OK. So, Mary, what do you think of the big event coming up?"

"Hugh, it's all happened so fast. The import of it is just now getting to me. I mean we're talking about Jesus coming back like it's Michael

Jordan making another basket…you know? Jesus is coming again. I wasn't even sure he was here the first time. It's phenomenal. (Suddenly, she downshifts to dejected). It's a circus here…so human. It's hard to describe. I can't image what sort of impact, if any, this will have on the world."

"We sure need something, don't we Mary?"

"Yes. What are they doing in New York for the event?"

"Let's see…they've got the Jumbotron in Times Square set to carry it, the baseball games are putting it on their screens and delaying their start times to carry it. It'll be a live feed world-wide…Internet; the whole bit. I'm just praying for the best."

"Hugh, you always want the best. Thanks. I'll talk to you soon. God Bless."

"God Bless you, Mary."

Mary's head is swimming with the possibilities. She wonders, 'Is this the answer? Stay here? Marry Michael? Have a kid? Do a show from here? That would be cool!' For the first time she's admitting that she just might Love the guy. Hey, it's just a matter of commitment, right?

"Michael? Mary…"

"I know who you are…

"Michael, can you come over?"

"Well, yeah. I could be there in a few minutes."

"I think I Love you."

Rappini on Fresh?
Baked Garlic Chips

You'll have to ask the baker about 'fresh' baked chips. Use day (or so) old garlic French bread if 'chips' unavailable. The crisper the better.

Steam bunch rappini in 1-cup water seasoned with olive oil, garlic (fresh grated or strong powdered) and black pepper. Use rappini leaves and flowers.

Cool to room temp and serve on the chips. Delish.

CHAPTER NINE

Thus Sprach Jesu

The hour is come. The collective eye of the enormous throng is drawn to a whirlwind waterspout swirling just off shore in the bay. As its well-contained intensity approaches some feel fear; all feel great anticipation. It sweeps onto land at the point of the cross. It is only a prelude, as a sailor's eye would've caught. Behind it is a huge fogbank. An ominous gray cloud that stretches from horizon to horizon and from heaven to earth. A cloud as dense and real as that which enveloped Sinai at the first revelation. As the fog pushes toward shore; from the watery cloud emerges a figure that seems to be held, hovering, slightly above the level of the ground. The figure is a well built human form with ruddy complexion and hair that is slicked back; as if wetted. His arms are open to welcome. The figure is hazy; but real...multi-dimensional. Like a hologram. The figure speaks,

"Peace be unto you, my brethren!

I come after he who preceded me, to fulfill the prophecy.

I come again to clarify the will of our Creator.

Never did I say to worship me...or my Mother.

All prayers are to God alone.

Erase the symbols of idolatry which you have erected and to which you pray.

Crosses and statues and saints will not help you.

When the angels come, it is God's will that they come.

The message has always remained constant. Why, from it, do you deviate?

What is the message?

It is that you praise God with all your heart and soul and all your mind.

This is your purpose on earth.

This alone will bring you peace.

Will you see God while you live?

Miracles surround you everyday; you have but to open your eyes.

The entire miracle of creation should stun you everyday in it's magnificence.

Worship not the image of God, but worship the attributes of God.

In your hearts, you know what is good and what is right.

Listen for that still, small voice inside that is constantly echoing eternal truth.

I appear here near what you call 'The Fountain of Youth'.

I am come to you as The Fountain of Truth.

If you have ever believed that God is, then you must believe that God is in all.

When you meet a fellow human, acknowledge that part that is of God.

For surely, if you cannot Love your fellow human that you see; how can you Love God that is unseen?

Do you remember the message I brought? Love one another as God Loves You!

Do not lose your soul; for this is possible.

Evil-doers will be punished; in this life or the next.

Only your Creator knows when this day will come. Be ready.

One day of atonement a year is good. Far better to be at-one everyday of every year. God is merciful; but do not take advantage. God knows the sincerity of your prayers…your heart.

I am come among you for the final time.

Hear the message. The eternal message.

Submit to the will of God to establish a new earth whose truth will mirror heaven.

Shirk not, this simple command that seems so difficult for you.

Worship God. My Lord and Your Lord.

Worship God in all that you do. Ask for guidance in the will of God in even the simplest of acts. All is important. All can be so much easier to bear.

In all things, observe moderation. Become obsessed by nothing in this world.

Love one another and praise God. Now, go in Peace."

With these words and a sound like a vacuum being filled, the cloud dissolves and Jesus is no longer in holographic suspension. His feet touch the ground. For the first time, it is plain to see that he wears a simple white V-neck shirt and jeans as he makes his way through the crowd in human form. The crowd parts. Most simply make way for him with mouths open as if jaws are unhinged. Many seem to not recognize him as the figure which delivered God's simple wish for us. Some gaze in awe; their chests swell in recognition of their witness. They understand. They will praise God in all that they do. Others seem disappointed that their religion, apparently, must be somewhat off the mark. Can they adjust? Is what they have seen real? Doubts will set in quickly. A human tendency.

Jesus walks calmly to where Skates is standing with Father Leonard and Sister Grace. Father Leonard has removed his collar. Grace has pulled her cowl; revealing beautiful flowing red hair. They have both removed their crosses. "It seems you have understood". Jesus remarks to the newly liberated pair. "The message seems so simple. It's so easy to believe. I think we'll live our lives more honestly now", says Leonard as he squeezes the hand of Grace.

Now, Jesus turns to Skates,

"Son, what are you doing the next few years?"

"What would you have me do, Sir?"

"I've got some traveling to do. I'd like to a have a companion. Are you interested in coming along for the ride? Actually, I could use some help driving, too."

"I can't see how I could possibly refuse," Skates responds with some new found maturity. He's been truly moved to have his inner intuitions verified by this 'miracle' today.

Mary is holding her microphone and trying to speak; but she's crying with joy at the same time. This state is rendering her live-remote to be nearly unintelligible. Michael doesn't immediately notice. His attention has focused on a distant figure in the crowd. He sees Marsilius Sandile kneeling and weeping into his open palms. He can't bring himself to aim his camera at him. Maybe he won't be a good newsman. Jesus, maybe he could be an **ethical** newsman and use words, in place of pictures, to convey emotions too private for film. Momentarily, as his concentration is lost and Mary's blithering, the folks at home get a true taste of chaos, as there is no picture and only intermittent babbling. In the sea of bodies, which this field has become, a voice confidently announces in Michael's ear, "I'm going to Trinidad!" It's Suffian. Another suddenly liberated soul. And he ain't talking about the Caribbean. Mose is making his way toward the temporarily inept pair just as Mary seems to faint. This snaps Michael back to 'here'. (Be where when?)

"Mose, you ever handled two at once?"

"I'm sure you mean 'cameras' and 'no', I haven't. But, give it to me; there's always a first time for everything-as we just witnessed!"

Mary's woozy. Michael motions to her to give the mike to him. He knows the best way for her to recover is to be interviewed. Although he's unaware of it; this will be his first on-air live interview ever, (with his future co-anchor) and it's national! All he's concerned with is helping this woman for whom he's developed great Love.

"Mary, can you describe the feelings Jesus words have had on you?"

"Oh, Michael, all my life I have prayed for clarification of how we should live. Do we follow this path or that ritual. What are we here for? Now, that message has been delivered…distilled. And it's so simple! Love one another and Love God in all that you do. Can you imagine…", she says—still half delirious with profound joy. She speaks through her delirium with a smile so broad it very nearly bursts the sides of her face even as she tastes the sweetness of her salty tears streaming down and some angle and feel their way into her mouth,

"Can you imagine? If everyone greeted each other in peace and wishes only peace for that person, how this world would change. No one would be able to do wrong. Certainly not for long. If we put away our differences and see that the wonder of creation is not ourselves; but the Creator. If we simply recognize the part of God that is in all—the world would change almost overnight. I can't continue. Praise God. This is Maria Diana Magdelena (she reaches to take back the mike) reporting live from San Jacinto, Florida. The Fountain of Truth. Peace be with you." At the wrap, Michael grabs her and hugs her in a seemingly endless, powerful embrace motivated by true Love of the highest dimension. Mose keeps rolling.

Somewhere in New Jersey, Mary's parents are in front of their TV. Two people in their 70's, down on their knees, praying the rosary with a statue of the virgin on top of their console. They Love their daughter, they Love Jesus, they Love God, this is what they do.

Baker is by himself in a corner of the grassy area behind the olive trees. Elisha is hugging him. Soothing his furrowed brow. He looks troubled; as if he's just been condemned to an ever-lasting death. Elilsha speaks words of comfort,

"I shall never leave you."

"I know. Th-thank you. But…what are we going to do?" TG realizes he can no longer take Gods or Jesus' name in vain. He feels that he must somehow atone for all the evil he has done in the name of God.

"Elisha, I wasn't always bad. But now I know just how far I've strayed. I have stolen...in the name of God. I've looked the other way while Tabarnac did...God knows what."

Tabarnac materializes behind them,

"Old man, never say anything of what I've done to anyone! Understand!"

Elisha boldly turns and asserts,

"Evil man. We've listened to you for years...and I don't blame you for that. But, God really does know what's what. And now we must stop. We don't have to tell anyone anything about you. The only one who matters already knows. No more can we be in business."

Tabarnac stares at them with eyes of death. Rain begins to fall. The sky darkens. It blocks the sun. Rain pours down from heaven. Elisha tries to cover her shaken mate with her body and guides him away from Tabarnac saying,

"Go in Peace."

"Fuck you, whore!" Tabarnac barks and begins walking toward the street as the rain intensifies. The crowd disperses to seek shelter from the storm. Most of the news crews have been distracted enough to not even follow Jesus. And now that they're looking around trying to find him; he's nowhere to be seen. Michael realizes Skates has, also, left the area. Moses, with a well-developed 'story' sense, allows his camera to follow Tabarnac up the walk; away from the cross. A humbling crack of thunder causes Moses to swing his camera back around at the instant that a bolt of lightning strikes at the base of the cross. It shears loose the huge column and it begins to fall toward the only human left in its free-fall path. Events of this nature are never in slo-mo, as many films depict. No. This is a frozen moment of crystal clarity; of distinct definition. It is as if all excess universal energy is concentrated right here-right now. And...it is unstoppable. The vertex of the crossbeam pounds Tabarnac into the pavement leaving a black lump oozing from its edges underneath the immense weight. Instinctively, Moses keeps filming as he and

Michael and Mary run to see if the evil blackness that was Tabarnac can be saved. Michael shoves the bulk of the weight from the battered body and twists it to see if the face still breathes life. He looks into eyes black as coal,

"Tabarnac, call on God to help you. Call on God to receive your soul!"

Unlike Rasputin, the first furious blow has done its work. Tabarnac does not stir. Michael can barely look at this sight, not because it is so bloody horrifying, but because he has never seen in death something which retains its evil aura so strongly.

Baker and Elisha scurry up to the scene as Michael again turns to the evil face on the ground and says,

"Go with God."

As the appearance of Jesus was carried live around the world, it is interesting to note some of the immediate re-actions. At Camden Yards there was a deafening silence during the broadcast as peoples attention had been focused on the large screen in the outfield. As soon as Jesus finished speaking the telecast was cut off. The crowd witnessed none of the aftermath, none of the commentary nor any of the cross-to-bear that befell Tabarnac. Shortly after the screen went blank, the cry of 'Play ball!' rang out. Except for a few people who left the stadium, it was simply another summer day.

The new U.S. president delivered a live statement shortly after the broadcast and the obligatory hour of analysis had ended. He said,

"Fellow Americans, surely we can take heart from this message of peace we have just heard; and what harm can it do to greet each other in peace. However, I have received information that this is possibly a hoax perpetrated by Islamic fundamentalists seeking to undermine our Judeo-Christian heritage. Not that there is anything wrong with Muslims. But I have been given intelligence reports that indicate that the physical appearance of this man and some of the wording used by him are modeling along lines that would fulfill a Koranic prophesy regarding the end of the world. Therefore, I would urge you not to be deceived nor to abandon your faith too quickly. We will be investigating and we will issue a full report when all the facts are known. Have a peaceful summer."

This, of course, was followed by another hour of in depth analysis.

From France,

"We have just witnessed a man, obviously American, claiming to be the Son of God. While his words seem to be benign and reflect an apparent sincerity, it is simply too little and too soon to abandon our Mother Church. Many miracles have occurred on our own soil. So what if America now has its' miracle. And what of this flagrant slap in our face? This man 'Tabarnac'? Merdeces Tabarnac. Obviously a cursing condemnation with French reference…and he is crushed on worldwide TV. We shall wait."

From Afghanistan,

"The American devils have concocted this jinn to deceive us into putting down our weapons and abandoning the fight for Islam. The Qur'aan demands that true believers accept Prophet Muhammad as the last prophet and the Qur'aan as the only unbroken word of Allah. Prophet Muhammad said that Jesus' coming would precede the Day of Judgment and that we shall know him. I do not know him. He has not fought for Islam, killed the pig or cancelled the tax. He **cannot** be who he claims to be. Peace be unto your house. Death to the infidel!"

From the democratically elected government of Russia,

"Peace Comrade Citizens. Today the religions of old that contributed so much to keeping our people in serfdom for generations have had the truth told about them by Gods own son. The revolution of our fathers and grandfathers against false gods has been vindicated. There is a God; as we all knew in our hearts. But there is no church; only church of the Spirit! This is where I will worship from now on. Peace upon the land!"

From the Holy Father in Rome,

"He did descend from the clouds in power and glory. But, from whither...and to what end? I have prayed for Jesus' return all my life. I cannot condemn him that I have not met. I will send an emissary; although I have found out that the priest of the Church of the Appearance is, at present, unavailable to assist us...I *would* like to meet this man."

Many more leaders from many nations and disciplines remarked on the telecast. Some were hesitant, cautious. Some outright condemned the good spiel. Some waffled (as is the custom of politicians). Those who are most happy have no 'collective' voice. These are ordinary people; good people that rarely, if ever, confessed their innermost beliefs to anyone. Many of these are members of churches, synagogues, mosques and temples who had joined because they believe in goodness, and in God...and in man. They had no other means of expression but the socially ordained outlets to publicly let their own desire for goodness show. These are people of **all** colors and situations who would, at the nearest opportunity, begin greeting their fellow humans with 'Peace', 'Peace be unto you and yours', 'Peace within your house' and a hundred other variations of the greeting Jesus ordained this day. We are nothing, if not diverse.

CHAPTER TEN

Jesus in My Living Room

The day after the event of Jesus' deliverance, Michael comes home after spending the night at Mary's hotel.

"Hey, Skates. Where are you, man?"

Michael's exuberantly walking through the house toward the sound of his sons voice. Michael's taking off his jacket as Skates sleepily exits his room in his boxers while wiping his freshly showered head with a towel,

"Hey Dad, did you have a good time last night?"

"The best, man-the-best. Sorry if I left you alone last night."

"Oh, don't worry. I wasn't alone."

Michael smiles shyly; thinking he knows what his son means.

"Skates…back in a minute. Gotta pee."

"Dad, you better use mine."

"Your what?" Michael thinks he hears running water coming from *his* bathroom

"Is somebody in my bathroom?"

"Yeah Dad."

"Who?"

"You won't believe it."

"Skates, you know I don't like you to have people use my room…"

"Trust me, Dad. It's OK."

Just then, Michael's bedroom door opens and out walks Jesus…in jeans and t-shirt cleaning his ears with a hand towel,

"Michael, don't be angry with the boy. He let me stay in your bed last night. I hope you don't mind."

"Mind? I think I'll have it bronzed!"

Michael is compelled to hug him. It is received as a natural human act.

"Michael, I'd like to borrow your son for a while."

"What do you mean?"

"I want him to go with me."

"Where?"

"I'm going to take some time to travel around the earth…talk to people. I'd like him to go with me. What do you say?"

"Skates, you OK with this?"

"Dad, I can hardly wait."

"Could be dangerous, you know…"

"Yes. But how could I resist?"

"I couldn't."

"Your job will be here, Michael."

"What job?"

"With the TV show."

"You mean…that's going to happen?"

"I do believe."

"Wow, that's great. What about you guys?"

"It'll be a road show…the Jesus and Skates World Tour", Jesus amuses himself.

"Amazing. Absolutely amazing."

"Listen, we'll need a car."

"What do you want?"

"Do you have something like Mary's?"

"I don't know why, but I think one will turn up."

"Good. Do you think you could get me some personalized plates?"

Sangre de Cristo Punch

Get a gigantic container that can be covered and refrigerated. Get huge bottles of White Zinfandel and Cabernet-Merlot blend.

Cut variety of fresh fruits into various shapes. Use strawberries, pineapples, kiwis, oranges, thinly sliced apples, cantaloupes and pears. Also add juice only of a few limes.

Mix wine and fruit together and allow to marinate for 2-3 days.

Serve in tall wine glasses with fondue forks for eating the succulent fruit.

Arrange for designated drivers and the rest of you just party on…

Chapter 10 sub-1
Lightweight

Michael has decided that on his follow-up visit to the doctors, he won't be surprised by having his weight mis-interpreted by the idiotic policy of weighing people with whatever clothes and assorted encumbrances they may be wearing. Besides, he has been very conscious of things going into his body. He is wearing only a tank top, cotton shorts and flip-flops. As he parks near Dr. Daniels' office, he shuts off his engine and stuffs his wallet beneath the floor mat. He holds his keys in his hands so that he can merely deposit them on a near by table at the moment he mounts the scale. Before he even picks up a magazine; the short stubby nurse with the cute voice calls him,

"Mr. Wade, come on in. Let's see how this diet worked for you. Step right up, will you?"

Michael slips off the flip-flops, tosses his keys onto a table and lays his sunglasses next to them as he daringly, confidently steps upon the scale. The nurse adjusts the weights on the top bar and glances at her chart. Then she double checks her balances and says,

"Mr. Wade. You've done great things!" (He thinks-'If she only knew...')

"Thank you. What does it say?"

"You've lost 20 pounds...and it hasn't even been that long. I've got to tell Doctor about this. Doctor, Doctor...", she goes in search of the good doctor. A few moments later she returns and instructs Michael to enter a waiting room while the doctor finishes his present business. Michael does so and begins his custom of perusing all written words in the small room to stave off feelings of captivity. He bends down to read a label on a jar and recognizes the doctor's voice outside the door,

"We're doing all we can to push this new drug…believe me, I'd love to have that bonus you're paying this month."

The voice that responds to the doctor sounds as if it must belong to a fairly young female…a drug company rep, he figures.

"Doctor, we'd love for you to *have* that bonus. I've got to move 20,000 units this month and anything you can do *will* be rewarded. Let me know when you need more!"

"I sure will. See you soon."

The waiting room door opens and the doctor steps in and says,

"Mr. Wade, congratulations. Twen-ty pounds! Fantastic! You're definitely going into the book. Maybe I'll call it the 'Cadillac Diet.' Can I count you in?"

"As long as I get credit. It seems I may be having something to do with a TV show soon and I'd like my name to get around…for any positive thing."

"If that's true, you're name might even help my book, sure, you can get your name included. Listen, do you ever have any allergy problems?"

"I guess I sneeze a few times when pollen's in the air…why?"

"I'd like you to try this Flucotanosine. You just inhale it once a day and you'll never sneeze again."

"Is that healthy-you could back up and explode?"

"Well, you should read this little book. Are your kidneys strong?"

"I guess. Jeez, this book is six pages with teeny tiny print. What can it do to me?"

"Not much. FDA approved…that's justa bunch of medical jargon. Read it over. Anyway, you're definitely going in the book. Congratulations."

Michael leaves and sits in his car thinking,

'This is so weird. First, Mr. H takes credit for his Cadillac diet; when it was Whitey. Then the doctor takes credit for his Cadillac diet; and it was me. Jesus comes and delivers the Word and gives the credit to God. Bizarre.'

The Lamb Lies Down Stew

Eire-Tec Version

Cut about 1 lb. lamb stew meat into small pieces. Retain the bone and include when cooking. In large cast iron skillet (with cover), sauté lamb in 1 tbsp. grapeseed oil. As it's cooking, add the following.

2 med potatoes cut up small

2 carrots cut up small

1 St. Augustine Sweet onion cut in strips

and ½ lb. mushroom pieces.

Mix and add ½ quart low-fart fatified skim milk. Also add 3-4 bay leaves and sprinkle with thyme. Cover and simmer slowly (an hour or more 'til milk is almost gone). Then add a generous sprinkling of sesame seeds and some peppercorns. Continue simmering until milk disappears. Serve over rice with raisins plumped in water and walnuts and freshly sliced mangoes and pears.

Epilogue

Jesus and Skates

Michael is kneeling to fasten a new license plate to a beautiful white, vintage Cadillac parked on the sand at the edge of the beach. Jesus wanted to take delivery at a remote spot to stay out of the spotlight for a while. Skates is loading gear from Michael's trunk into the Caddy as Mary and Jesus look on. When the last screw is driven, Jesus speaks,

"Thanks, Michael…", he turns to include Mary and places a hand on their shoulders saying,

"I want you to be very happy."

His hand drops to Mary's belly, which he gently rubs.

"Take care of this new life; he will be important to the world."

Mary is stunned; but elated…and not altogether surprised. She throws her arms around Michael and hugs him. Some dreams come true. Michael turns to Skates,

"Let me know how you're doing…OK? I Love you very, very much."

Jesus tosses the keys to Skates and says,

"You better drive. I don't quite have the hang of it, yet."

As Jesus and Skates mount their chariot, Michael speaks,

"Thank you, Jesus. Take care of my son. I Love you both."

With that, Jesus and Skates pull away and head up A1A. It's a bright, clear day. The ocean is at their right and the sun overhead. Michael and Mary follow them for a short distance before they swing left back to the mainland. Their last view is of the white Caddy, top down, heading north with Jesus' hair blowing gently and Skates at the wheel. Michael wonders if the cryptic tag inscription is a clue as to where they're heading...

HNGR 84

On the bumper is an altered version of a sticker Michael had seen earlier.

GOD   IS   RELIGION

HalleluJah Jambalaya
Gumbo File' Filet

❀

(Note-the word 'gumbo' derives from an African word for okra. There is no okra in this recipe. I had none; so, I used what I had. Also, I dislike using refined flour; but, it's the simplest way to make a roux for thickening sauces.) Read entire recipe before you begin.

Heat ¼ inch grapeseed oil in large cast iron skillet. As it's heating, add 1 packet of Old Bay Seasoning, a generous sprinkling of file' powder. 4 fresh pliable large bay leaves and 2 tbsp. flour.

Have ready the following:

1 huge St. Augustine Sweet onion chopped (with chives)

1 large red or green bell pepper chopped fine

1 long hot pepper chopped (seeds and all)

3 chopped garlic cloves

1-2lbs. canned Italian tomatoes, cut up

2 tbsp. red wine vinegar

bottle of Burgundy

juice of 2 limes

1lb. Texas brown shrimp (shell on)

4 small cod filets, cut up

a bit more flour

To the sauce of the first paragraph, add the red wine vinegar and 1 glass Burgundy. I always drink one, as well. Add the lime juice and 2 more tsp. file' powder. Add the veggies (onion, bell pepper and hot pepper) and garlic. Add the cod and tomatoes. Cook for a couple of minutes and add the shrimp. I like the shell on for two reasons. You can slurp the juice from them and approximate the Louisiana crayfish experience and you can dip the peeled shrimp in the curried mayo described below. Cook until shrimp are pink.

Now, using about 3 tbsp. flour, make a roux by slowly stirring hot water into the flour until it is a thin paste. Stir into mixture a little at a time until it thickens.

You could serve this over rice, but I don't.

Curried Mayo for Dipping

To your desired volume of the mayonnaise of your choice, add (to taste) a mess of strong curry powder and (again, it's all to taste) some hot sauce. I use a capful of Redfields Anguillan hot sauce. Mix and chill 'til serving. Great on the above shrimp.

Bibliography

Hochelaga-The name Native Americans gave to the village that became Montreal. The name of the Timucuan village that became St. Augustine was Seloy. Some say Seloy was the chiefs name. Hochelaga means (loosely) 'wide spot in the water'.

Father Lenny-modeled after a real friend of mine. A priest who married a nun.

Jesse Rod-Jesse is the modern version of the ancient name-Jesus. Jesus was of the House of Rod.

Deir Sunbol-a village near the site of some rubble that is regarded as the actual house of Abraham, who started it all.

Bulbs of the Vestibule-A newly named portion of the female anatomy.

Sandile-Last great chief of the Zhosa tribe of South Africa.

Ben Asher-There are about 25 such names in the Encyclopedia Hebraica-this refers to one of the most ancient Hebrew scholars.

Tom Jude-Tom as in 'doubting Thomas'-Jude as in Judas or Judea.

Merdeces Tabarnac-A bastardization of Quebecois slang that loosely translates to 'shit is fuck'.

Room 316-John 3:16

Hangar 84-The area at area 51 where the alien bodies were kept, if you know what I mean…

Made in the USA
Columbia, SC
30 June 2020